IMMORTAL IRIS

IMMORTAL IRIS

REGULUS-ANTHONY KELLY

To Nico. Thank you for every moment we spent together in your too-short time on Earth. And to Kawa, the sister I never knew I needed until I had.

TRIGGER WARNINGS

This book does not contain any explicit sexual content, however it does contain the following potentially triggering topics.

- Sexual violence
- Suicide
- Pregnancy and abortions
- Drug use and overdosing
- Eating Disorders
- Self-Harm
- Emotional abuse
- Homophobia/transphobia

Please use caution when reading, and be mindful that these topics can spring up at any time. If any of them hit home for you, remember that you are not alone. There's a whole network of people like you, and you'll find them when you need them most. Together, healing will happen for all of us.

PRELUDE: SEEDS

There were only a few things that Keoghan Winchester could not stand, but she hated those things with every fiber of her being. Her childhood home, for one. Every moment that she was inside it, she felt her throat constrict and her heart race in fear of hearing the clicking of her mother's heels on the stone floor. She needed to escape just as much as she needed to breathe, perhaps more.

The chance came in college applications. Her family lived in up-state New York, so she applied to every college on the West Coast that her parents approved of. With bated breath, she waited, waited, waited. Finally, her acceptance letter at Stanford University arrived, and she packed her things.

When she stepped onto campus, she had one extra piece of bag-gage- her cousin Lukas Lancaster, whose family lived a town away from hers. Both the Winchester and Lancaster families prided them-selves on money, status, and appearance, creating a similar environ-ment for Lukas as had been for Keoghan. She remembered an incident where Lukas's father was in her house, dragging Lukas away from her after hearing that she was cutting her hair.

"She'll look like a lesbian," Keoghan remembered him saying. *"We can't have our son be associated with those people."*

Years later, Lukas had come out to her as gay. He had been terri-fied- *"You're the only person I can tell, Keo. My parents- my father would kill me. My friends would tell him. Please, Keo, say that I can trust you with this. Please."*

"You can trust me, Reg. I promise. This will stay between us."

Lukas smiled and shook his head. "Will you ever stop calling me that?"
"Never."

As Keoghan and Lukas entered their residence hall, she placed a hand on his shoulder and looked up to give him a small smile. His blue eyes were clouded with fear, barely visible through his messy blonde hair.

"We're free, Lukas."

He nodded, but grimaced. "Free, yet still so reliant on our parents."

"We're an entire landmass away," Keoghan told him. "Forget about them until we need to see them again."

"I'll try my best," He sighed, running a hand through his hair. "Let's go to our rooms, 'kay? I'll see you later."

"See ya, Reg. Text me everything you want to tell me about your roommate. And tell me if you fuck. I know that's supposed to happen at some point."

Lukas's eyes seemed to pop out of his head. "Jesus- fuck, Keo?"

Keoghan laughed, and Lukas rolled his eyes.

"Alright. Bye, Keo."

"Bye, Reg. The Jester loves you."

They parted, and Keoghan took the stairs to her floor. It was the top floor of the hall, and she hoped for a good view. Counting the numbers on the doors, she stopped in front of hers.

"306," she whispered. "Room 306."

The start of her new life. She opened the door and stepped inside. There was a bathroom off to the side of the door, and beyond it a cozy room with two beds, two closets, and two desks. Another person stood in front of the bed closest to the door. Keoghan took in their appearance, and took note of their similarities and differences. Their skin was a bronze tone, hair dyed a bright orange and eyes a chocolate brown. They were an average height and wore a cashmere yellow sweater and black jeans with black and white Converse. Keoghan's skin was also tanned and her hair dyed, but only partially- her bangs were a blood red while the rest of her hair was a deep chocolate. The main difference between them was her eyes- Keoghan's eyes were a piercing green. Keoghan was also significantly smaller than them, something she knew she shouldn't be proud of but was anyway.

"Hey!" the person greeted. "I'm Eri. Are you my roommate?"

Keoghan nodded slowly. "Room 306?"

"Yeah."

"Sweet, then yes. I'm Keoghan."

The door was flung open, and two people who vaguely resembled Eri entered. "Eri! Here are the rest of your things!"

Keoghan looked between them. "Are you...?"

"We're Eri's parents," the woman introduced. "Are you their roommate?"

"Yes!" Keoghan smiled.

"Oh, lovely. Where are your parents, honey?"

The smile vanished. "In New York."

The man set a box down. "They couldn't make it?"

"Didn't want to. Besides, I'd prefer if they weren't here. We..."

"I get it. I lost contact with my mother when I was 19," the man nodded. "Well, Eri, be your roommate's family. The best relationships are formed in college."

Eri smiled. "I will. Keoghan, do you want to come to dinner with us?"

Keoghan looked at them in confusion and slight panic. "Me? Dinner with your family?"

"Of course," their mother cut in. "You're very welcome."

Something inside Keoghan cracked. This family was unlike any she'd seen before. They were kind. They were genuine. They... they cared. She had never experienced anything remotely similar, even as a young child.

She wondered if their restaurant behavior would be different, too.

"Keoghan, you'll be getting the salad. No dressing," her mother told her.

Keoghan nodded. "Alright."

"You've gotten so fat. How many calories did you eat yesterday?"

"800."

"It must be the carbs. Ask for no croutons. And light cheese."

"I'll gladly go with you, then," Keogham smiled, pushing away all her thoughts. It was fine. She could go to a restaurant. "Thank you."

ACT ONE: SHOOTS

1

The first thing Keoghan saw when she entered her Statistics classroom was a fiery redhead in a loud debate with a Chinese woman in the front of the classroom.

"I'm telling you, it's making it more efficient!" the redhead argued.

"It *also* creates a wider allowance for workplace discrimination. Most resumes that it's fed are men's, and there have been cases where it's discriminated against women simply for being women."

"But it got fixed."

"That's entirely beside the point. Who says that it was fixed? The people who made it?"

"Okay, who else would say that it was fixed-"

Keoghan stepped closer to the women. "Another AI debate?"

"Well, what else? It's part of life, you know,," the redhead responded.

"Yeah, I understand, but I just feel like the debate of 'should we, shouldn't we' is getting old. We all know it's going to be used, so we should be debating regulations and ways to safely incorporate it instead."

Both women nodded, considering her statement. The redhead smiled and extended her hand.

"I've decided I like you. My name is Celena Asher, and I'm your friend now."

Not to be outdone, the other woman stepped forward. "We *both* are. Iris Song, pleased to be your friend."

Keoghan smiled, but her head was whirling. Friends? So soon? Did they truly think she was good enough to associate with? It didn't matter. She had friends.

"I'm Keoghan Winchester. It's nice to meet you both, Celena and Iris."

Celena shook Keoghan's hand vigorously. She had a firm grip, which Keoghan wasn't expecting, and she could see muscles flexing through Celena's sleeveless hoodie when she moved. Her flame-toned hair was up in space buns, and her pale skin was covered in freckles, accenting her deep blue eyes. Keoghan's eyes flicked to her sharp eyebrows, the right brow decorated with a pink ring piercing. She was lean, and something in Keoghan screamed jealousy. Keoghan wondered if Celena was judging her. She had to be looking so fat. Maybe she should have worn baggier pants.

Iris took her turn shaking Keoghan's hand, and Keoghan took in her appearance. She was tall, with porcelain skin and black hair in a pixie cut, a small streak dyed a night-sky blue. A pair of round glasses sat on her nose, and her black eyes sparkled. Keoghan smiled as she saw that the woman wasn't as muscular as Celena. She felt bad judging their bodies, but it had become a habit for her. She had to compare herself, had to shame herself.

"I assume you're a Business major as well?" Iris asked.

Keoghan nodded. "Of course."

"I intend to take over my family's tech company when I graduate," Iris informed her. "Are you planning on any specific job?"

"I'm from New York, and my aunt lives in the City working at an advertising company that I'll probably work at."

Celena crossed her arms. "I don't have any connections. I'm looking to forge my own path."

Iris did not comment. Keoghan, however, nodded.

"I think that's cool," she smiled. "Any idea what direction?"

"Sports. Something with soccer, maybe."

"Are you sure a Business major is the right path for that?" Iris asked. "Maybe you would do better in a sports med program. Or nutrition."

"I'm here on a soccer scholarship, actually," Celena told her. "Business was the major my parents wanted."

Iris nodded slowly. "I see."

"I was considering nutrition," Keoghan said. "My family wanted Business as well."

Keoghan looked around; most students were already seated. There were three seats in the middle of the lecture hall that were open, so they made their way over to them and sat down. She placed her laptop on the desk in front of her and focused her eyes on the professor. It was time to begin.

Keoghan, Iris, and Celena planned to meet for lunch with their roommates in one large group. It took a bit of group-texting and compromising to decide on a spot, but they eventually decided on a coffee shop. When she arrived, Keoghan saw Iris sitting with a girl she presumed was her roommate. The girl had rosy skin with blonde hair in a bob, accented with purple streaks. She wore a black lacy tank top underneath a distressed black and green cardigan, as well as black cargo pants. Iris looked quite different in her starry blouse and slacks.

Keoghan dragged her nails across her arm when she was close enough to see the woman's build. She was wraith-thin.

God. She was probably judging Keoghan right now, thinking about how fat she was, how horrible, how greedy she would be when she ate, how–

"Keoghan!" Iris smiled. "This is Chloe Maxwell, my roommate. She's a Psych major."

Keoghan sunk her nails into her skin, forced a return smile, and sat down next to Iris. "Hey, Chloe. I'm Keoghan Winchester."

Just then, Celena arrived with another girl. She was tall, with long brown hair and hazel eyes. Her outfit was also a contrast to Celena (who was still wearing the muscle hoodie), as she was dressed in an almond sweater vest and brown skirt. Keoghan exhaled as she saw her. Thank God. She wasn't nearly as thin as Chloe.

"Hey, Kay," Celena greeted. "Meet Elizabeth. She's the coolest English major that was ever created, which isn't hard to do because English majors are mildly terrifying."

"Creative writing or lit English?" Eri's voice asked from behind Elizabeth.

"Creative writing," Elizabeth responded. "Although I am interested in lit."

Eri nodded. "Fuck yeah. Hey, roommate.."

"Nice to see you, Eri, " Keoghan responded. "I'm going to go order."

Those who had not ordered followed her into the coffee shop and up to the counter. Keoghan looked at the menu. No calories listed. Fuck.

"I'd like a- uh..." Keoghan's voice trailed off as she saw the barista. He was a tall man with long mousy brown hair and beautiful hazel eyes, and something about him radiated kindness.

"Take your time," he smiled.

"I'll have a... a... an almond milk latte? Unsweetened if you have that type of milk. Thank you."

The barista rang her up, and she looked at his name tag. *William.*

Jesus fuck.

Even his name was pretty.

As she waited for her drink, she stole glances at William. The way he moved- everything was intentional. He spoke softly, yet directly, and she swore he looked back at her a few times.

Once everyone had their orders, the group sat back down at their outdoor table. They introduced themselves to those who did not know them, and then broke into conversation. Keoghan hoped that nobody would notice her pulling out her phone to log the almond milk. She logged sweetened, just in case. Fuck. She should have gotten black.

"What are you doing?" Celena asked.

Celena seemed like a safe person to tell about her calorie tracking. She played sports, she had to be safe.

"I'm, uh, tracking my drink," Keoghan told her.

Celena nodded. "The horrors of being healthy, hmm?"

"Yeah," Keoghan laughed quietly. "Healthy."

"Your daughter has lost forty pounds in the last six months," her doctor told her mother. "She was at a healthy weight before, and now she's underweight. Do you know why?"

"We keep our family healthy," her mother responded. "She didn't look healthy when she was that large. She still doesn't."

Keoghan absent-mindedly looped her fingers around her wrist. She felt fat. Her mother knew she was fat. Her doctor would tell her to keep losing weight. She was horrible.

She decided to lower her calorie limit again.

"Earth to Kay," Celena smiled. "You good?"

Keoghan nodded. "Yeah. I'm good."

"Good. Because if you zone out, your friends here might draw a mustache on you."

Friends. Keoghan smiled. She had friends.

"Just not in Sharpie, please," she laughed.

2

"There is much to be said in silence," Keoghan read aloud, "for silence is the mother of all communication."

Her first two weeks at Stanford had gone by in a coffee-shop-barista-staring-filled blur, but she thrived. Classwork was hard, all-nighters were pulled, but she thrived. Well, as much as she could. Her brain fog was as bad as usual, and she had found herself on the brink of fainting several times.

Still, she loved Stanford. Her English class, a requirement, was one of her favorites; she genuinely enjoyed essays for the first time.

When the class was dismissed, she walked to the coffee shop to meet with Iris and Eri for a Physics homework session (Eri was a Physics major, so the two women would be relying on their enjoyment of the subject to get them through the class). She was the first to arrive, so she stood near the counter, waiting.

"Almond milk girl!" she heard a voice call. When she looked in the direction of its origin, she saw William waving her over. "C'mere."

Heat rising to her cheeks, she strode over to him. "Yeah?"

"Who are you waiting for?"

She instantly cooled off. He didn't want to talk to her. He just wanted to know why she wasn't buying anything.

"My roommate and friend," she responded.

"Are they coming soon?"

"They should be..."

A twinkle appeared in his eye. "Far enough away that I can buy you a drink on my break first?"

Keoghan's eyes widened, and she nodded. "I'm sure we can manage."

William motioned for Keoghan to follow him and led her to a back room. "I've never seen you around here before."

"I'm a Freshman," Keoghan admitted.

"Senior," he nodded. "Engineering major."

"Business."

Smiling, he pointed to a small vending machine. "I can't buy you a coffee because I'm not forcing my coworker to make one, but I can buy you a lovely Diet Coke."

"Eh, sounds fine," Keoghan laughed. Diet. Good. "Thanks, by the way."

"Of course. It's not every day I get to buy a drink for a pretty girl."

Keoghan blushed, but something felt off. He was a Senior. He was at least twenty-two years old. She was eighteen. That was the same difference between a teenager and a child under the age of ten. Still... it was college. There was no reason it shouldn't be okay. Right?

Right?

It didn't matter. He thought she was pretty.

Nobody thought she was pretty except for him.

"What the fuck."

Iris was staring at Keoghan incredulously.

"What?" Keoghan asked.

"That is. Not okay. A fucking Senior should not be buying you drinks and flirting with you."

"I'm eighteen," Keoghan argued. "It's fine."

Eri shook their head. "It absolutely is not. That could end horribly in so many ways."

"But it won't! He's so sweet, and he asked me to come to his place on Saturday."

Iris and Eri's eyes widened.

"Do not go," Iris warned. "Seriously. Do not."

Eri nodded in agreement. "That is not safe."

"It's fine, I promise. He wouldn't hurt me," Keoghan told them. "He's not that kind of guy."

"One of us will be waiting outside after you go in. You have to be safe, Keoghan," Eri responded. "You cannot just blindly trust men."

"What happened to *you*, then? I know I shouldn't, but he's not like other guys."

Eri's expression soured. "You wanna know what happened to me? I was assaulted at fourteen by not one but two guys I met at school who were nice to me and bought me things and were, in my naive mind, the nicest boys on Planet Earth. *You have to be careful.*"

Keoghan shook her head. "You're overreacting. I'm sorry about your trauma, but you don't get to dictate my choices."

"One of us will be outside. End of story."

"Kay, I really fucking hope you're not seriously thinking of going through with this," Celena said as the two women walked to one of their classes. "You met this man, what, two weeks ago?"

"Oh my God, I cannot have this conversation again. Why can't someone be happy for me?" Keoghan groaned.

"Kay. Dude. This is the most bullshit rape plan I've ever heard. I'd be happy for you if he was, I don't know, your roommate or something, but this random-ass guy? Seriously?"

"He's not random! I- Jesus fuck, alright. I'll stop asking for happiness from my friends."

Celena rolled her eyes. "Don't you dare try to guilt-trip me, Kay. I'm trying to keep you safe, and so are Iris and Eri who, by the way, asked me to stand guard outside his door."

"You?" Keoghan asked, surprised. Celena stopped in her tracks.

"Look at this."

She flexed, and suddenly sculpted muscles appeared out of her otherwise normal-looking arm. Keoghan stared at her arms and felt the urge to measure her own with her fingers.

"Sleeper build, man," she told Keoghan. "And it's not just for show. I'm a Third-Degree Black Belt in Tae Kwon Do."

3

Keoghan arrived at William's place at exactly 6PM, the time they had decided on. He opened the door and led her inside, where a twelve-pack of beer greeted them. They cracked open cans and reclined on the couch. After talking, a second and third can had been emptied. Keoghan had attempted to track them, but had given up after her second. It could be a metabolism day.

"So, you're doing stuff in New York?" William asked.

"Yeah," Keoghan smiled. "I'm not from the City, though. I think I'll end up working there regardless."

"Cool. I'm going into bioengineering."

"Sweet."

William leaned over and smirked at her. "You know, you're probably the most mature Freshman I know."

Keoghan giggled- had she ever giggled before?- and tucked a strand of hair behind her ear. "Does that make you immature, then?"

"Could an immature man kiss like this?"

Before Keoghan could react, he was on top of her and kissing her violently. She struggled beneath him, she couldn't breathe, it felt *wrong*.

"Come on, you said you wanted it when we talked about meeting," William told Keoghan, his hands wandering lower on her body. "Don't be a pussy and back out. You'll be so good for me."

"I-"

She was cut off as he kissed her again, pulling her into him. She pushed herself away, somewhat getting him off of her, stood up, and began to put on her jacket.

"I'm leaving."

William grabbed her wrist and pulled her back. "No, you aren't. You don't get to leave."

"HELP!" Keoghan called, to no avail. She was indoors.

"Shut. The fuck. Up. You came here asking for it, so you're going to get just what you wanted."

"Leave me alone!"

With her free hand, she slapped William across the face and used his stunned state to knee his groin. He doubled over in pain, letting her go in the process, and she grabbed her purse to leave.

"Fuck you, whore-ass bitch! You're going to fucking regret this!" he called as she ran out the door, tears streaming down her face and her arms wrapped around herself. Her eyes stung. Her hand stung. But most of all, her heart ached.

As soon as she crossed into the street, Celena came out from the bushes.

"I told you, dude. Did he kiss you against your will?"

Keoghan nodded.

"Touch you?"

Keoghan nodded.

"Go further?"

"I got out," Keoghan whispered. "I feel so fucking stupid."

Celena wrapped an arm around Keoghan's shoulder. "It's okay. We all do stupid shit sometimes. I'm just sorry that your stupid shit was this. Let's get in the car."

She walked Keoghan to the passenger side and opened the door. Keoghan got in and leaned her head against the window, staring out of it.

"Did something like this ever happen to you?" she asked Celena.

Celena nodded slowly. "My first boyfriend in high school. I... I don't want to get into details. I'm sorry."

"No, it's okay. I don't think I want to get into details, either."

Keoghan felt a pat on her shoulder and jumped. Her heart was pounding. Her muscles were tensed. She couldn't relax even though she knew she was safe.

"This isn't even my car," Celena began. Keoghan knew she was just talking to make sure she couldn't spend enough time with her thoughts, but she appreciated it. "It's Iris's. I'm borrowing it for tonight. I like it, though. It's a nice Subaru."

"The gay car," Keoghan murmured.

"We're all gay here," Celena laughed.

"I'm not," Keoghan responded. "At least, I don't think I am."

"You've got time. We're just 18. We have years ahead of us."

"Yeah."

They arrived at Keoghan's residence hall, and Celena parked. "I'll walk you to your dorm."

"It's okay-"

"*I'll walk you to your dorm.*"

Exiting the car, Keoghan reached for Celena's hand. "Thank you."

Celena squeezed Keoghan's. "No need. Friends look out for each other."

Once they entered Keoghan's room, Celena wrapped her into a hug.

"You're safe now, Kay. We're not going to let anything happen to you."

Keoghan did not go to the coffee shop again for the next two weeks. She avoided every building where an Engineer could be. Still, she did not feel safe. She never went anywhere without a friend. She bought a self-defense keychain. Still, she did not feel safe. She punished herself for being so naive, so stupid. She lived on black coffee.

One evening, she and Eri walked the dreaded route past the coffee shop. Despite herself, Keoghan cast a glance through the window. William stood in the window, and upon recognizing her smiled wide. He pulled something out from his pocket, held it up, and the window turned red as an echoing bang crashed through Keoghan's ears.

Keoghan felt her vision blur, and then the world blinked away.

4

Two months into her college experience, Keoghan had lived a life beyond her wildest nightmares. Despite everything, she attended her classes. She hung out with her friends. Everything could be normal if she told herself it was. Her friends attempted to talk about what happened, but she refused every time. Talking about it would mean that what happened wasn't normal. That *she* wasn't normal. And the only thing Keoghan wanted was to be normal.

Deep down, she knew she wasn't. She wasn't eating. She was barely sleeping. She was shaking all the time, passing out. She didn't even want to *think* about her heart rate.

One afternoon, Lukas knocked on her dorm door. "That coffee shop you loved is open again. Wanna go?"

Every inch of Keoghan's body turned cold, every nerve alert, every fiber of her heart pulsing as fast as it could without killing her. She couldn't go back there. She couldn't. Every time she saw it out of the corner of her vision, the horrible sight of William's grin before he killed himself assaulted her mind. With that frontal assault came the reinforcement troops of everything that he had done to her- everything that he could have done if she hadn't made it out. She could have been raped. She could have been killed.

But maybe he *was* right. Maybe she *was* asking for it. She responded to his advances. She let him buy her drinks, talk to her, she didn't fight back immediately when he assaulted her.

Maybe it was all her fault.

"Keo?" she heard Lukas's voice say. "You good?"

Keoghan nodded quickly. "Yeah. I'm good. I, uh, don't feel like coffee."

"Let's go into town, then. There's an amazing grill close to campus."

"Alright," Keoghan whispered. Fuck.

Lukas looked her over, and a gleam of suspicion appeared in his eyes. "You're not telling me something."

"What- What do you mean?" Keoghan stuttered. "I'm-"

"Family intuition, Keo. You know we basically have twin telepathy."

Keoghan sighed. "It's..."

She began to shake, and tears pricked at her eyes. Balling her fist, she repeated the age-old mantra to herself: *I will not cry. I will not be weak. I will not lower myself to giving into emotion.*

Lukas clasped his hand over hers and gave her a gentle smile. "You can tell me about it over lunch. Let's go."

Nodding, Keoghan used her free hand to blot at her eyes without smudging her makeup. "I'll try."

Keoghan ordered an unsweetened iced tea. Nico got a reuben sandwich. Once his food was served and their drinks refilled, Lukas looked Keoghan dead in the eye.

"You need to tell me what happened. I know it has something to do with that coffee shop."

Keoghan broke away from the eye contact to look into her food. "It's a long story. And I don't know if you want to hear it. I don't know if I'm ready to talk about it."

"Keo," Lukas said firmly, "I know you. I know your parents gave you the same bullshit treatment as mine. One thing I learned about living in secrecy is that it'll eat away at you. I thought I wasn't ready to come out. I kept it inside until I nearly killed myself over it. You need to tell me what happened before it comes for your life."

Keoghan looked up. She hadn't known that Lukas had gotten so low in his depression. He never told her. Instantly, she wanted to ask him why. She could have helped. She could have done something.

But she was doing the same thing. He was right. If she kept William a secret, she would follow him into the grave. And she couldn't do that. She couldn't leave Lukas alone.

"I, uh... I met this guy at the coffee shop," she began slowly. "He was a Senior. I didn't know that at first, so I went and stared at him a lot. Eventually, he kind of asked me out. We hung out. I flirted with him. He flirted with me. He invited me to his place. And then he..."

Her breath was beginning to come out in rapid shudders as she felt her heart rate increase. Her limbs felt like they were overheating. Her face felt numb. She couldn't talk about it. She couldn't form any more words. She couldn't think. She couldn't-

Lukas's hand covered hers, and she saw him stand up and walk over. He wrapped her into a hug, his strong arms providing pressure to her chest. They didn't hug often, so it took Keoghan by surprise, but she could think again. Her breathing slowed. Her heart slowed. Slowly, her limbs weren't boiling anymore.

"I'm so fucking sorry," Lukas murmured into her ear. "I'll kill him."

"He took care of that already," Keoghan laughed lowly. "Blasted his head open right as I was walking by."

Lukas's grip tightened- "*That guy?*"- and he shook his head. "You didn't deserve that, Keo."

"Maybe I did," she whimpered, tears beginning to cascade down her face. "Maybe I was asking for it. Maybe I secretly wanted it. Maybe-"

"No, you did not. You did not deserve it. You were not asking for it, and you *certainly* didn't want it. End of story."

"Reg, I hate myself for it. It was all my fault."

"Keo. Stop fucking with your own head. You're the least at fault for the fact that that *dickhead* couldn't keep it in his pants, and even more the least at fault for his suicide."

Sniffing, Keoghan leaned her head against his shoulder. "I can't believe that. I know that somehow it was my fault."

"I will tell you this as much as you need to hear it. You are not at fault," Lukas told her. "And I will stand here for as long as you need to feel safe."

"You can eat now. I'm safe."

"You sure?" Lukas asked.

Keoghan nodded. "Yeah."

Lukas gave her one last squeeze and then let go, sitting down in front of his food. "I know you're not eating again."

"Leave it, Reg," Keoghan warned.

Lukas shook his head. "No. I don't want you to get sent away again."

Keoghan grimaced. In her Freshman year of high school, her doctor had sent her to an inpatient facility for eating disorders. Her mother had protested, but she had been told that if she didn't let Keoghan go, the doctor would call CPS.

"I'm fine," Keoghan told him. "I know what I'm doing. I have it all under control."

"That's what people who are going to kill themselves with their habits say."

"I'm not going to do that. Seriously, Reg, just leave it."

Lukas sighed. "Alright. But I'm not going to forget about it."

5

Keoghan stood in front of the mirror in her bathroom, naked. In front of her sat a scale, laughing at her, taunting her. She knew she had to be quick; Eri would be coming back soon and the scale was noisy.

Gingerly, she stepped on the plate, afraid to break it as always.

90.1 lbs

Running a hand through her hair, Keoghan bit her lip and shoved the scale back into a corner. She had gained weight, but how? She meticulously tracked her calories, ate in the range she had deemed acceptable... Was the 'starvation mode' she saw people on Tumblr debunk actually real?

Sighing, she put on her clothes- a sapphire sweater and black ripped jeans- and exited the bathroom.

"Fuck my life," she cursed under her breath.

October arrived, and the Halloween spirit swept across the campus. Every popular cafe had pumpkin everything, professors had candy buckets in their office hours, and the talk of the friend group was costumes.

"We should totally be sexy businesswomen," Celena told Iris and Keoghan one day. Iris nodded, considering it, but Keoghan froze. She thought she had gotten over it, but she couldn't bring herself to dress provocatively. She didn't want any more male attention.

Noticing her distress, Iris bumped their shoulders together. "Or sexy businesswomen and their male overlord, Daddy Keoghan."

"I'd be down for that," Keoghan laughed, the freeze fading from her. "I'll buy a fake mustache."

Celena nodded. "I have my suit from Junior Prom that you can borrow. It might be a bit big, though."

"I'll wear it, as long as you tell me that it has sleeves."

"What do you think I am, a barbarian?"

"...Does that mean there aren't sleeves?"

"No. It has sleeves."

"Good."

Keoghan, Celena, and Iris went shopping for their costumes a day later, going to Spirit Halloween in Redwood City after a detour at a corner store to get Celena a new vape.

"Oh my God, look at this," Celena cried as they walked into the adult costume section. "It's a fucking hotdog."

Iris laughed. "You gonna wear that?"

"You could put lingerie over it," Keoghan added, feeling all the tension of the prior days evaporate from her shoulders. "Or make it into a crop top."

"Haven't seen you really smile in a bit," Celena noticed. "That's good, Kay. Maybe I will be a sexy hotdog."

"You could actually do that," Iris nodded. "We can be ketchup and mustard."

"Yeah, on second thought, I'm not going to be a hot dog. Come on, let's look for mustaches for Kay's costume. Or, or or or! Kay could be Einstein and the two of us sexy atoms!"

Laughing along, Keoghan felt at ease for the first time since William. She was safe. She was with her friends. They were accommodating her.

Maybe everything would be okay.

A few days later, Keoghan received a text from Elizabeth.

Wanna meet for coffee (with Chloe) at the cafe near the English department?

Keoghan smiled. She didn't know Elizabeth well, even less than she knew Chloe, but any friend's invitation out would be good.

[Of course. What time?]

Keoghan's black denim jacket fanned in the wind behind her as she approached the cafe. Her hair would do the same, had it not been braided. She had been planning on attempting heatless curls, and a braid seemed like a good place to start. It had been falling out more recently, and she wanted to hide how much it was thinning.

Elizabeth and Chloe sat at a table with a maroon umbrella, and when she sat down they pushed a to-go cup over to her.

"I figured you wouldn't want what you used to get," Elizabeth told her. "I got a pumpkin spice latte but with oat milk."

Keoghan forced a smile. How many calories were in a pumpkin spice latte? And oat milk? It probably was sweetened, so it had at least 120 per cup. How much did they use? Fuck. Fuck, fuck, fuck.

"Thank you, Liv. May I call you Liv?" she asked. A nickname. Good. She could hide everything. She just had to pretend to be normal.

Elizabeth nodded. "Yes. And of course. I heard *him* call you a name based on the drink, and I wanted to make sure I didn't make things worse. I know how bad things like this can get."

"I really appreciate that."

Keoghan did. Even though the drink was causing her panic, she knew it came from good intentions.

Chloe took a sip of her black coffee and gestured toward Elizabeth. "We met in high school, right after something similar happened to me."

"Have all of my friends had this happen?" Keoghan wondered aloud.

"Not everybody," Elizabeth responded. "But it is a lot more common than I thought before I met Chloe."

"81 percent," Chloe murmured, shaking her head. "81 percent of women."

Keoghan nodded slowly. "Fuck, man."

"Exactly."

A silence.

"I just want you to know that it's okay to talk to someone professional," Chloe told her. "My therapist helped me manage my PTSD because of it. She also helped me learn skills for BPD and, uh, an eating disorder. Especially now, while the mental scars are so fresh, I'd honestly recommend it."

Keoghan nodded. She wanted to ask about the eating disorder, but knew it would be rude. "Therapy. That does sound like a good idea."

"It's really helpful, I promise. Having someone to just talk to is amazing, even if you don't get any diagnoses or learn any skills."

"God, I need to get a job. I can't keep living off my parents' money forever."

Elizabeth smiled and pulled out a piece of paper. "I was saving this for whomever needed it. It's not great, but it's something."

Keoghan took the paper and read it. *Now Hiring! East Campus Convenience Store.*

"I think it's time I went to the East Campus Convenience Store."

Application. Wait. Interview. Wait. Wait. Wait. Wait. Wait.

You're Hired!

Keoghan's first day at work passed quickly. The manager trained her on the system and watched her as she did her best to do her job. When her shift was over, she received a pat on the back and a "Good job".

Chloe texted Keoghan one afternoon.

Hey

We should talk

Come to my dorm

Keoghan sent back a thumbs-up, slightly confused. What would she want to talk about? Could it be their shared disordered behavior? Did she see through Keoghan's disguise? Could she be wanting to tell Keoghan that she was too fat to have an eating disorder? Keoghan knew it was irrational, but she couldn't help but believe it. She wasn't sick enough to be sent back anywhere, not that she wanted to be, but God, she had to. She had to be sick enough. She needed it in her bones.

When she arrived at Chloe's dorm, Chloe was waiting in front. Music was playing softly, a song that Keoghan recognized but didn't think Chloe would listen to.

"Climb up the H of the Hollywood sign, in these stolen moments the world is mine..."

"Hey, Keoghan," Chloe greeted. "I wanted to talk to you."

Keoghan nodded. "I gleaned that."

"Okay. This is going to sound really out of pocket and rude, but... are you anorexic?"

Keoghan knew it was coming. What should she say? What... she had to come clean. She had to tell someone who wasn't Lukas, someone who could understand and relate.

"Yes. I was diagnosed in ninth grade."

"We're the masters of our own fate, we're the captains of our souls..."

Chloe gave her a small smile. "Me, too. I just... I wanted to ask, because I want a buddy. I want someone who will relate to me."

"Yeah. I don't want to be your toxic internet motivation buddy, though," Keoghan told her. "I don't think we should be motivating each other to get worse. My body is enough motivation already."

"Keoghan... you're already so fucking skinny," Chloe sighed. "And I know the whole point is that you can't see it, but you are. And I'm... I'm trying to get help. Liza- Elizabeth- is worried. She says I'm going to die. And I don't want you to die, either, because you're skinnier than I am."

"And I was like: take off, take off, take off all your clothes..."

"I don't want to get sent away," Keoghan murmured.

"I know. Talk to your therapist once you meet her."

Keoghan nodded. "I will. You, too, though."

"Yeah. I will."

"They say only the good die young, that just ain't right 'cause we're having too much fun, too much fun tonight..."

Chloe offered a small smile. "Do you want to come in?"

"Uh, sure," Keoghan responded.

"Should I turn off my music?"

"No, no. I didn't expect you to be into Lana, though."

"Yeah," Chloe laughed. "I'm usually an alt bitch, but Lana is my exception."

"And a lust for life, and a lust for life keeps us alive, keeps us alive..."

Keoghan sat down on the floor, Chloe next to her and her back against a wall. "How do you deal with... anorexia?"

Chloe grimaced. "By telling people I'm recovering and then doing all the same shit that I did before, just in a less restrictive manner."

"Do you think there's ever hope for recovery? For you or for me?" Keoghan asked, tilting her head back. "Because I don't. I think that once it's in you, you can't get the disorder out. No matter how many times you get sent away, it always comes back."

"That's about where I'm at, too," Chloe sighed. "I've been in programs before, but all that's happened is force-feeding and pretending to be better to get out."

"God, the world is bleak..."

"You can say that again."

"And a lust for life, a lust for life keeps us alive, keeps us alive..."

The two women sat there for a long while, saying nothing. Chloe leaned her head on Keoghan's shoulder, and Keoghan closed her eyes.

Chloe couldn't die.

She just couldn't.

Halloween inched closer, and so did Keoghan's therapy intake session. It would be scheduled two days before the holiday. She couldn't wait to see if she liked the therapist that had been recommended for her- a specialist in sexual assault trauma. Her name was Soledad, and her office was just outside of the campus. Keoghan wondered if she had ever met another of William's victims, if he had any. That matter tore her in two- she wanted to have another woman to relate to, to tell her that it gets better, but she didn't want William to have hurt anyone else. If he hadn't gone to the length he had with her, if he hadn't killed himself after the other women were taken, it meant they must have given in. They must have let him violate them, strip them of their autonomy, condemn them to a life of even worse trauma than what Keoghan had gone through. Their trauma must have been worse. She hadn't been raped like they would have been. She had escaped.

He had shot himself in front of her.

But she hadn't been raped.

That thought followed her throughout her days, looming over her like a black cloud in a sunny sky. It could either go away, or more could gather around it.

Keoghan tossed and turned in bed, restless. She tried laying on her back. Her stomach. Moving her hand. Curling into a ball. Stretching. Nothing put her to sleep.

"Hello, almond milk girl."

Instantly, she shot up in bed. "What the fuck?"

William appeared out of the shadows of her room and stalked closer to her.

"Can't sleep, huh?" he purred. *"That's what happens when you kill some-one."*

"I didn't fucking kill you. Leave me alone," she cried.

He chuckled and shook his head, leaning over her and tracing an ice-cold finger along her jawline. *"Oh, but you did. If only you had given in. Kissed me back. I killed myself because of you, almond milk girl. This is all. Your. Fault."*

Keoghan pushed his hand away and shook her head. "Leave me alone!"

"I'm going to fucking kill you, you know. I'm going to stand here, in your room, every night until you see my eyes everywhere. And then, then when you wonder if you'll ever fall asleep again, I'm going to take my aim and hit you right in your forehead with the same gun I took my own life with."

"Leave me ALONE!"

Keoghan's scream pierced William through his chest, and he shattered. When all the pieces hit the ground, she saw Eri staring at her from their bed.

"Keoghan, are you okay? You started screaming in your sleep."

She raked a hand through her hair, breathing heavily. "I will be okay. I just had a nightmare."

"Was it... him?" they whispered. Keoghan nodded.

"He told me he was going to kill me."

"I'm not going to let that happen. You scream, I wake up. If anyone tries to get you, I'll fight them."

Keoghan offered them a small smile, though she didn't know if they could see it in the dark. "Thank you, Eri."

"Anytime.."

6

Keoghan and Lukas sat in the bed of a truck belonging to one of Lukas's friends, sipping beer. The friend was a lesbian woman Lukas had met in one of his classes, and she had invited them out to go stargazing in a nearby dark-sky community. Music was playing on her speaker, and Keoghan watched Lukas as he drank can after can.

"I'd be the last to say that I've got problems, embarrassed to admit that I can't solve them..."

"You good, Reg?" Keoghan asked. "Slow down a bit."

Lukas shook his head. "No. I don't drink much, so let me get wasted."

"That- your not drinking is why you should slow down."

"Goddamn, baby, you drink like Hemingway, but your writing's no good and your songs all sound the same..."

Lukas tossed his third can into the truckbed next to him and reached for another, but Keoghan slapped his hand away.

"Nuh-uh. You're cut off."

"You're not my mother, Keo," Lukas snapped. "Let me do my thing."

Keoghan took his hand and looked him in the eye. "Are you alright? You seem wild tonight. What happened?"

Lukas sighed. "I... I don't know. I just feel like shit. I feel nothing. Drinking makes me feel happy, or, at least pseudo-happy. That's more than I get normally."

"I get that. But seriously, slow down. You're gonna make yourself sick," Keoghan told him gently.

"You better give up this act, you don't know how to play, and come back down before it's too late. You need to come back down 'cause this isn't safe..."

Lukas's friend leaned against the truck and smirked at Keoghan. "You're not lookin' at the sky, hun."

Keoghan laughed gently. "Just playing the role of Lukas's mother."

"Hey, I mean, I ain't lookin' at the sky either. I've got a pretty gal here to keep my eye on."

"What?" Keoghan asked, slightly dumbfounded. "Where?"

"You, hun," she giggled.

Keoghan jerked back in confusion. "Me? I'm... I'm not... I'm not gay."

The woman smiled and hopped into the truckbed. "You're allowed to experiment, y'know. It's fuckin' college. Lukas's told me all about your family's bullshit, an' I think you gotta try things out."

Lukas smiled. "I'll go sit in the front seat, then. Have fun, Keo."

Taking a deep breath, Keoghan nodded and turned to the woman. "You know what? Maybe it's the alcohol... but fuck it. Sure."

Something about the woman's offer felt different than William. Maybe it was because she had asked, allowed Keoghan to give her consent. It could be the alcohol. Still, Keoghan knew it felt right. She was taking back her control of her autonomy.

"Let's do this," she told the woman.

"That's my girl," the woman laughed, leaning forward and kissing her. Keoghan marveled at how soft the woman's lips were, how she smelled like passionfruit, how her hands felt in Keoghan's hair. When the woman pulled away, Keoghan smiled.

"That's... damn."

The woman laughed again and booped Keoghan's nose. "Ah, I ain't gonna remember this tomorrow. It was nice kissin' ya, though... what's your name?"

Emboldened by the drinks she'd had, Keoghan smiled. "Nick. Yours?"

"My name's Cassidy. And, yeah. It was nice kissin' ya, Nick."

"Goddamn, baby, you drink like Hemingway..."

"Wanna do it again?" Cassidy murmured.

Keoghan's eyes widened, but her brain seemed to be on autopilot. She nodded. Cassidy took her hand and helped her out of the truckbed, walking behind a few trees near the vehicle. As soon as Keoghan couldn't see Lukas anymore, Cassidy's lips were on hers, moving kisses away from her lips, to her neck, to her collarbone... Keoghan felt a rush, ecstasy running through her body.

"You're a good girl, Nick," Cassidy giggled when Keoghan's fingers tightened in her hair. "And a damn good drinking buddy."

The next day, Keoghan woke up with a raging headache. Her dorm lights, usually low and comforting, felt jarring. The sounds of Eri shuffling around rang through her ears.

"What the fuck...?" she murmured.

Eri came over to her bed and smirked. "You got in pretty late last night, covered in lipstick."

"Wait- what the..." Keoghan's voice trailed off, and memories from the previous night came flooding in. Cassidy. Drinking with her. Kissing her. Going into the trees, the rush, the smell of her perfume.

"Fuck."

"Can I come up?" Eri asked. Keoghan nodded. "Alright. You're going to tell me everything that happened."

"Kay, what the fuck?" Celena laughed as she heard Keoghan's story. "You... you're not gay, right?"

Keoghan sighed. "I don't think I am. Iris, help..."

Iris, who sat next to the two women, had a look on her face that Keoghan couldn't place. It almost seemed like jealousy, but that couldn't be right. Why would Iris be jealous? Unless... she wanted to kiss Cassidy? She wanted to get drunk in her truckbed?

"It's all a thing you have to figure out on your own," Iris finally said, placing every word carefully. "But you'll get there. Eventually."

"I just... I can't believe I did that," Keoghan murmured, shaking her head. "After William... it was so soon. But I don't know. It felt... I think it was the alcohol."

Iris nodded. "Do you regret it?"

"No."

Celena took a pull from her vape and smiled. "Baby's first hookup... you get a hit to celebrate."

"I, uh..." Keoghan stammered. She wasn't sure if she wanted to try it or not. "Will I get addicted?"

"No," Celena smiled. "But you don't have to if you don't want to."

Keoghan nodded. "I want to."

Celena handed the pen to Keoghan, and she took a small hit. She coughed violently.

"I know, your first hit's always bad," Celena laughed. "But good job."

"Thanks," Keoghan laughed through coughs. "I don't think it's for me, though."

"Totally understandable."

Iris shook her head with a smile. "You either make the best or worst decisions."

"Oh, trust me, I know."

7

Keoghan and her friends met up a few days later at one of the dining halls. It was usually difficult to organize such meetings, as Celena was usually in the gym in her free time, Elizabeth slept late, and Chloe took so many classes that she had a thirty-minute window for lunch. Therefore, they decided to meet for dinner.

"Did you know," Celena was saying as Keoghan sat down with her food- a chicken breast with broccoli-, "that saying the word 'heck' is actually a combination of 'hell' and 'fuck'? So I decided that I'd just say 'what the fucking hell' instead. It's more appropriate."

Elizabeth giggled. "I do not think that's how it works, Celena."

"I'm doing it for the children, Liv."

"Since when do you care about kids?" Iris asked. "I seem to remember you saying 'fuck them kids' on more than one occasion."

"Well, maybe I'll keep the kids alive so they can go fuck themselves."

"How would they die-"

"Shh, shh. I'm keeping them all alive."

Finally, Keoghan's therapy intake date arrived, and she took her bicycle to the office. It was a two-story building made of brick with white shutters and flowerboxes on the windows. She locked her bike to the small rack outside and entered. As soon as she sat down in the powder-blue toned waiting room, her phone chimed with a request for her to check in. She completed the check-in form, and a woman she assumed to be Soledad entered two minutes later. The woman was tall and curvy with bronze skin and long braids accented with golden cuffs.

"Keoghan?" the woman asked, receiving a nod. "Great. Let's head to my office upstairs."

Keoghan stood up and followed the woman up the carpeted stairs, taking note that each room was a different pastel hue (some doors in the lower and upper hallways were open). Soledad's office was at the very end, and her room was a dusty rose.

"Sit wherever is comfortable for you," Soledad told her. Keoghan looked around the room; there were two plush chairs and a cloud-like sofa on opposite sides of a geode coffee table. There was also a desk with a rolling chair. She sat on one of the plush chairs, crossed her legs, and watched as Soledad closed the door and sat in the other.

"Welcome, Keoghan," Soledad smiled. "Is Keoghan your preferred name?"

Keoghan nodded. "It is. My cousin calls me Keo, though, and some of my friends call me Kay."

"Those are all very pretty names. Just double-checking, you said on your application that your pronouns are she/her?"

Keoghan nodded again. She wasn't used to being asked questions about her identity, as her parents expected her to be a perfect daughter. A perfect straight, cisgender daughter.

"Alright. Now, your application said that you had recently experienced sexual assault, and that the perpetrator committed suicide in front of you."

A third nod. "I wouldn't have made it out if my friends didn't... if they didn't care about me."

Soledad's eyes were soft, and she shook her head. "Nobody should be sexually assaulted, and nobody should experience, let alone watch, a suicide. To have both, especially from the same person... have you been experiencing any thoughts of suicide of your own?"

For a change, Keoghan shook her head. "Not at all. I have been thinking that it was my fault... and he showed up in my dream. He told me he was going to watch me and kill me."

"First of all, Keoghan, I want you to know that none of this was your fault. No matter what you wore, no matter what you said, you did not ask to be assaulted. You did not force him to commit suicide in public."

"Thank you. I don't know if I can believe that, though."

Soledad smiled gently. "We'll work on it. As for the dream, did you have any more like it?"

"No."

"How has your sleep been?"

Keoghan grimaced. She hadn't been sleeping much, as she had been terrified to see him again. Terrified to wake up with his bullet in her head, his eyes on her, his hands on her, his-

"Keoghan. Come back to me," she heard Soledad say.

Blinking, Keoghan sighed. "I'm sorry."

"No need to apologize. I just want to make sure you're in as little distress as possible in this volatile time of healing."

"I haven't been sleeping a lot," Keoghan admitted. "I'm scared. I'm scared of him. I'm scared of myself. I'm scared of feeling him. I'm scared of seeing him. I'm scared that my mind will bring him again because deep down I wanted it."

"I can't tell you how you feel," Soledad began, "but I can tell you that you most likely did not want him to touch you without your consent. As for your fear, I want to validate that. You have every right to be afraid. I'd like to work on building distress tolerance skills through the therapy modality of Dialectical Behavior Therapy, or DBT, with you, should you choose to see me long-term."

Once again, Keoghan nodded. "That sounds good."

"Alright. Would you like to talk about what happened now, or move on to paperwork?"

"Actually..." Keoghan sighed. "There's something else I have to talk about."

"Of course. What would you like to say?" Soledad asked.

"I... I have anorexia. And my friend said I have to get help."

Soledad smiled gently. "I will do my best to help you, but the real work comes from yourself. Disorders like that, they never truly go away. I'm sure you know this, but you have to consciously fight for your life back. Are you prepared to do that?"

Keoghan nodded. "Yes. Also... I'm sorry for dumping so much on you, but... I'm starting to wonder about my sexuality."

"You should be dumping this on me, I'm the person you should be talking to. Tell me about it."

"I..." Keoghan grimaced. "I kissed and, uh... I... kinda hooked up with... a woman a bit ago. And I'm so confused. I don't think I'm gay, but I don't know. And it felt so right, but so wrong because of William..."

Soledad nodded. "Identity is confusing, and it takes time. Let it develop, Keoghan. You don't want to rush yourself into labels."

"I don't want to be gay."

"How bad would it be if you were?"

Keoghan fell silent.

When Keoghan returned to campus, she was met with Lukas in her room, sitting in her desk chair.

"Eri let me in. I wanted to talk to you after your first therapy appointment."

Keoghan smiled and sat in Eri's chair. "Where is Eri?"

"A recitation got moved. How was it?" Lukas asked, leaning back in the chair.

"It went well. I'll meet Soledad once a week from now on."

Lukas nodded. "Good, good. I actually wanted to tell you something, too."

"I'm all ears."

"I... I have a boyfriend."

Keoghan's eyes seemed to pop out of her head. "Lukas, that's great! Who is he?"

"His name is Ben Johnson; you might have seen him in your class since he's a Business major."

"Sounds familiar. Oh my God, I'm so proud of you."

Lukas smiled. "I was hoping you'd react that way. I didn't know, but..."

"Of course I would be proud. You deserve this," Keoghan told him. "I want to meet him."

"He's gonna be at the Halloween party we're going to."

"Fuck yeah. God, I can't wait."

Music. Keoghan heard the music from several yards outside of the house the Halloween party was in. It was a mix of upbeat Halloween songs, and as she walked in she heard Ashnikko's "Halloweenie" begin. She clutched her small crossbody purse close to her side, Celena and Iris close behind her. Keoghan could smell Celena's vapor mixing with the stench of marijuana emanating from every corner of the room.

"You never had a love like me, you never hit a drug like me, fuck like me..."

"Where's everyone else?" Keoghan shouted over the pulsing music. "I don't see Eri and the others."

"Boo."

Keoghan jumped as she felt a tap on her shoulder. It was Chloe, dressed as something remotely similar to a scarecrow.

"Eri, Liza, and your cousin are in the kitchen with some guy. Let's go."

The three women followed Chloe to the kitchen, where the first thing Keoghan locked her eyes on was Ben. Ben, whose hand was draped over Eri's. Quickly, she pulled out her phone and snapped a picture.

"Trick or treat, I take my drinks neat, spank him if he talk a little too sweet..."

"Hey, Reg," Keoghan whispered, brushing her hand against his shoulder. "We need to talk."

She pulled him aside and pointed at Ben, whose free hand was tucking a curl behind Eri's ear.

"That is not your boyfriend."

Lukas grimaced. "So I may have overspoken. He said he was interested."

Keoghan groaned. "Je-sus, Reg."

"I'm sorry, Keo. I learned my lesson. I just... I got excited."

"He doesn't seem all that interested, you know."

"Yeah. I know," Lukas sighed. "But a guy can hope."

"She'll never eat the butt like me, only tricks for your ass, it's Halloween..."

"Hey, let's go back to the others. I'm sure Celena knows where the drinks are," Lukas told Keoghan, who nodded slowly.

"Never pegged you for the drinking type, but after the truck..."

"You must have pegged me wrong."

"Jesus fuck, do not say that," Keoghan laughed. "Alright, let's go."

They joined back with the larger group and sure enough, Celena was handing out Jell-O shots.

"To Halloween!" she shouted.

"To Halloween!" the group chorused. "Fuck yeah!"

Everyone took their shot, and Lukas took a second.

"I'm fine, sublime, like vines I climb into your window, write my name in blood on your pillows..."

Keoghan watched as Lukas reached for a can of beer and cracked it open. Why was he drinking so much again? It was bad enough when it happened in the truckbed, but a second time? Was he that upset about Ben? Was he lonely? Maybe she should spend more time with him. She studied his face- his smile and laugh seemed real, but his eyes were trained on her.

Was it her fault?

Fuck.

"Hey, you good?" she called to him. He nodded.

"Just worried you might want to leave."

"I will if you drink any more of those shitty beers."

He laughed and set his can down. "They are shitty."

"Hey, don't talk shit about my holy water," Celena told them.

"I thought that was vodka," Keoghan smiled.

"Ugh, Kay..."

"Make 'em kiss my ass like thank you, darling, my pussy pleaser is a pink Bugatti..."

Lukas reached for another shot.

Keoghan moved closer to him and bumped their shoulders together. "Are you upset about Ben?"

"Would you not be?"

"I would. I just wanted to know."

"I feel like- holy. Fucking-" Lukas cut himself off and left the room. Keoghan followed him, casting a brief glance back at where he had looked. Ben was holding Eri's waist, and from her perspective they seemed to be kissing.

8

Keoghan continued following Lukas as he strode away from the party, up the street, and to a bench under a streetlight.

"Leave me alone," he cried. Keoghan's heart felt as though it was breaking in two just watching her cousin hurt.

"I'm going to sit here with you," she told him. "You don't have to talk to me. I'm just going to make sure you're safe."

"I can handle myself."

"You were walking in a slalom. How much did you drink before I saw you?"

Silence.

"I just wanted to forget everything," Lukas whispered, voice quavering. "I'm so done, Keo."

Keoghan placed her hand over his and held it tightly. "You don't need to forget whatever happened by drinking, as good as that may sound. Talk to me, Reg. When I was assaulted, you told me to talk it through with you. I don't know what happened to you, but I'm here. I want you to rely on me, Reg. We're family."

Lukas sighed and leaned on her shoulder. "I don't even know what's going on."

"Did something happen?"

"Something's been happening my entire life. You know my parents. You know I'm gay. You know their views on that. And now, now when I get to college and I can finally live my own life, live without fear, my first crush tells me he'll date me and then goes and fucking kisses your roommate. And I know that doesn't explain why I was drinking earlier, but I don't know why I was. I just needed, I don't know, to forget everything. Forget my parents. Forget that... that I'm different."

"Being different-" Keoghan began, being cut off by Lukas.

"Is bad. I'm going to be a politician, Keo. Different is bad. Nobody will vote for me if I'm gay. I have to shove it back down, just like I did at home. I can't ever be who I want to be."

"You don't have to be a politician."

"Yes, I do. My father told me before I left that if I even consider doing anything he hasn't approved, he'll know and I'll no longer be his son," Lukas sobbed, eyes full of tears.

Keoghan wrapped her arms around him and held him tightly. "We'll figure something out. We'll get you out of this hellhole, Reg. I'll do everything in my power to make sure you get a future. I promise."

"Maybe I don't deserve a future."

"You deserve a future more than anyone else," Keoghan said firmly. "With someone who's better than Ben. Some pretty man named, I don't know, Louis."

"Louis?" Lukas laughed quietly. "Where the fuck did you get that name from?"

"It sounds sexy."

"No, it does not. Besides, I don't care about sex appeal. I want someone who is emotionally intelligent."

Keoghan nodded. "Looks like you've got your priorities straight."

"Or gay."

"Or gay."

Lukas sighed, and Keoghan wrapped her arm around him.

"Do you remember when you used to sing?" he murmured. "You thought you were going to be the next big star."

Keoghan laughed gently. "Hey, I was six."

"You sang for forever, though."

"I guess I did. I can't remember much of my childhood."

Lukas smiled. "You should sing for me."

"Okay, you're drunk," Keoghan chuckled. "I'm shit at it."

"Please?"

"Alright."

Keoghan sighed and began to sing quietly.

"I'm not afraid of anything at all, not dying in a fire, not being broke again..."

Lukas nestled his head into the crook of her neck. "Phoebe Bridgers..."

"Had nothing to prove, 'till you came into my life, gave me something to lose..."

"Keo, I love you," he murmured. "And I'm sorry if I ever leave you."

Keoghan stopped singing. "What?"

"I just... I don't know if I'm going to make it much longer."

"No," Keoghan said firmly, taking his hand. "You're going to live. You're drunk, that's why you're thinking this way. You're going to live."

"Mmmm..."

"Lukas. You have to live."

"Okay," he sighed. "I'll try."

"Hey, let's get you to your dorm," Keoghan told him. "It's getting late."

"Alright."

As they walked to the residence halls, Keoghan ruminated on what Lukas said. He had to live. She didn't know he had been feeling like dying, but... he had to live.

The next day, Keoghan woke up to find that Eri wasn't in their room. She rolled over to where her phone was (hung in the lofted bed by a long power cord) and sent them a text.

[Where tf are you]

[If you're with Ben I'm going to be personally responsible for your demise]

She set down her phone, but it chimed a few seconds later.

I'm sorry keoghan pls don't kill me

Keoghan groaned and banged her head against her pillow. Eri was breaking Lukas's heart. She loved them, but Lukas was family. A debate began in her mind. Should she tell Eri that Lukas liked Ben? She couldn't do that. She couldn't out Lukas. Should she let it happen? She couldn't do that, either.

[He's kinda a fuckboy yk]
It's just a fun thing for me
Don't ruin it.

Setting down her phone, Keoghan raked her hand through her hair. Shit.

"I don't know what to do," Keoghan said to Celena and Iris later in the day as they waited for class to begin. "Eri's putting me in a tough situation with... a friend."

"Do we know this friend?" Celena asked, taking a swig from her water bottle.

"Uh. No. Also, what's in there?"

Celena smirked. "A white Monster mixed with a Baja Blast Zero."

"Je-sus, Celena," Iris laughed. "You're going to give yourself a heart attack. Didn't you drink a Redbull at breakfast, too?"

"This bitch needs her fuel. It may be the off-season for soccer, but I still have to lift and stick to my team diet."

"God, sports sound like hell."

Keoghan didn't say that there didn't have to be a sport to feel like one was in food hell.

"They are, but I love it," Celena nodded. "Anyway, Kay, I think you should give seniority in this case. How long have you known this friend?"

Keoghan grimaced. "All my life. They're one of the closest friends I have."

"They take priority, then. Just because Eri's your roommate doesn't mean they get priority over them. What happened, anyway?"

"Just a small opinion issue. It's nothing," Keoghan lied. "Don't worry about it."

"I know you're lying, but I'll leave it," Celena told her. "You get to keep this private if you want."

"Nothing else, though," Iris joked.

"Exactly. You get to tell us everything else, including what you think about when you masturbate."

Keoghan stared at her incredulously. "Excuse me?"

"Kidding, Kay," Celena laughed. "God, the look on your face…"

A few days later, Elizabeth, Chloe, and Keoghan met at the same cafe they had previously to discuss Keoghan's venture into therapy. As usual, the other two women were there early, and Keoghan came to find a drink ready for her.

"Pumpkin's out now that it's November," Chloe told her. "Therefore, I present to you a rose tea. I… I didn't want to get you anything with milk."

Keoghan smiled and sat down. Chloe was helping her. "Thank you. Should I give you the money you spent back?"

"Nah, it's good. It's a special occasion!"

"Are you sure?"

"Of course," Chloe smiled. "Now, how was therapy?"

Keoghan took a drink from her latte and nodded. "It was good. Soledad was really approachable, and her office was comforting."

"I assume you're returning?" Elizabeth asked.

"I am," Keoghan affirmed. "We have weekly meetings set up on Thursdays."

Chloe reached over and squeezed Keoghan's hand. "You're going to heal, Keoghan. I have faith in you. All the faith."

"Thank you. I really hope I will."

"How's… how's our friend Ana doing?" Chloe asked.

Keoghan grimaced. "I'm trying. I… I've been eating again."

Chloe nodded. "I have as well. I think we can make it out of this, at least for a bit."

"I think we can, too."

What Keoghan didn't say was that it was only for appearances. Inside, she still couldn't stand the sight of her own body, imagined what she would look like if she were smaller, didn't want to take up space.

One of her worst fears was taking up space. Physical space, but also mental and emotional space. She didn't want to be a burden on anyone, nor did she want to be any larger than she had to in any way.

"Okay, I'm sorry, but I'm calling bullshit on you," Chloe sighed. "And I'm calling bullshit on myself. I don't know if we'll make it out. And I know you don't either. But I'm not calling bullshit on the fact that we can try."

Keoghan nodded, unconvinced. "Yeah... try."

That night, Keoghan stared at her ceiling. She couldn't sleep, despite the fact that she hadn't gotten a good night's rest since her dream about William. Sighing, she got up to use the restroom. As soon as she closed the door behind her, she felt a cold rush down her spine.

"Turn around, bitch."

No. No. Nonononono.

"Go away," she whimpered. "I don't want you here."

"I said, turn around."

She did, turning to face William's ghost. He cracked a manic smile and grabbed her neck, pressing her against the sink and mirror. Leaning over her, she felt his icy aura penetrate her skin.

"You'll be so good for me."

Keoghan struggled in his grip, but he began to choke her. Breath cut out of her lungs, she felt faint, she tried to scream but couldn't.

"I'm going to take you right here, and then, little almond bitch, I'm going to kill you."

If Keoghan was scared before, she was terrified now. Her vision began to blur, she tried to pry his fingers away from her throat, she felt him press closer and closer, the door opened.

"Keoghan!" Eri cried.

Keoghan's vision returned. William was gone. She was lying on the floor of the bathroom, and her head spun.

"You fell. Are you okay? Do I need to take you to the med center?"

"I saw him," Keoghan whispered. "He choked me and threatened to rape and kill me."

Eri knelt down and wrapped their arms around her. "I'm so sorry. I'm so, so sorry."

"Eri, I'm scared," Keoghan sobbed. "He's coming after me. I can't sleep anymore. I can't stay awake. I'm never going to escape him."

"You will escape him," Eri told her firmly. "He won't come after you forever. I promise."

9

Soledad smiled at Keoghan, who stared at the floor. "How has your week been, Keoghan?"

Keoghan raked a hand through her hair. "He won't go away," she whispered, voice breaking. "He won't leave me alone."

"William, I presume?"

"Yeah," Keoghan nodded.

"How has he been staying around?"

"I see him. I'm just... doing whatever, trying to sleep, and he shows up. I feel his cold body, I hear him threatening to rape and kill me, I can't escape him."

Her breath began to come out in rapid, shallow gasps and she felt her heart pound. "I can't. I can't anymore."

"Keoghan, breathe with me," Soledad told her. "One, two, in. One, two, hold. One, two, out."

"One, two... fuck," Keoghan panted. "Fuck, fuck, fuck."

"Keoghan. Come back to me, Keoghan."

Soledad's voice was distant, far too distant. Keoghan felt her vision blur, flash white, and then fade into black.

"Keoghan."

Keoghan blinked. Everything was a dusty rose.

"Keoghan, can you hear me?"

That was Soledad speaking.

"I... I can hear you," Keoghan mumbled, slowly lifting her head. She sat in a chair in Soledad's office, head spinning.

"You blacked out," Soledad said gently. "Are you feeling alright?"

"I'm..."

"I think we should end the session early. You need to get home," Soledad told her.

"Alright," Keoghan responded, massaging her forehead. "Sorry, Soledad."

"It's no problem. We have lots to talk about, but right now may not be the best time."

Keoghan nodded. "That makes sense. Thank you."

"Of course. Stay here as long as you need to feel safe."

Keoghan exhaled and settled into her chair, sitting in silence with Soledad for the rest of the hour..

Keoghan and Iris walked to class together a few days later, leaving a sick Celena in the dorms. They were tasked with sending her notes from class and making sure she didn't fall too far behind.

"It's so weird spending time together without Celena," Iris commented. "I don't hate it, though."

Nodding, Keoghan stretched her arms upward to relieve tension in her shoulders. "It is, but I think the same. Maybe we could do it more often."

"That would be amazing. Maybe we could study together in the library after class?"

"Sounds great," Keoghan smiled.

"It's a date, then! Your last class ends at 2:30, right?"

Keoghan nodded, though she was distracted at Iris calling their meetup a date. She knew it wasn't meant in the romantic sense, but she felt her heart flutter as if it was.

What the fuck?

First off, she wasn't gay. Second, she was not in the space for romance. She couldn't be in the space for romance, not with the memory of William so fresh.

But Iris wouldn't hurt her.

But it wasn't a date.

And she was definitely not gay.

Right?

Keoghan met Iris in the library at 2:40. They had reserved a study room earlier in the day so they could talk while working without disturbing the other students.

"It's so wild that it's November," Iris sighed as she furiously typed a project progress report. "The semester's gonna be over soon."

"Fuuuuck," Keoghan groaned. "I'm not ready for that."

"Are you going home for break?"

"Absolutely fucking not. I'm staying as far away from New York as I can."

Iris nodded. "That's fair. I know we're not, like, super close friends, but if you want to come to mine, you can."

"Really?" Keoghan asked, eyes lighting up.

"Yeah. My family's great, and they'd love to meet you. I, uh, talk about you. Just a bit."

"I would love that. Thank you, Iris."

"Of course," Iris smiled. "I don't want you rotting in school over Christmas."

Thursday sped closer and closer until, finally, it arrived. Keoghan slogged her way through her classes, looking forward to seeing Soledad. When she eventually locked her bike in front of the office, she breathed a sigh of relief. It was time to take care of herself.

Soledad stood in the waiting room as soon as Keoghan entered, and they headed through the pastel hues of the building to her office. Keoghan looked at the different seating options, but none of them felt right. She couldn't sit in a chair any longer, and the couch seemed too soft.

"May I lay on the floor?" she asked quietly.

Soledad smiled and nodded. "I want you to feel comfortable, so you can sit wherever and however you want."

"Thank you," Keoghan responded, lowering herself to the ground and stretching out. The fluffy pink carpet welcomed her, and she breathed a sigh of comfort.

"How has your week been?" Soledad asked. "I'd like to do a trauma assessment today, but only after we discuss any events. I'd also like to talk about what happened last week."

Running a hand through her hair, Keoghan sighed. "Alright. My week... I don't know, it was good, I think. I just... I'm having a bit of an identity crisis. Still. I... I know this girl, and we went on this study date thing, and I got way too happy about it. I don't... I don't want to be gay. I know I said that last time, but... I really don't want to be gay."

It was the second time she said it out loud, but it felt like a new wound. She knew there was nothing wrong with being gay, but she couldn't handle keeping it a secret from her family. She didn't want to go through what Lukas had to.

Soledad nodded. "I see. Why don't you want to be gay?"

"My family... my cousin is gay, and he had to keep it a secret for so many years until it nearly killed him. I can't go through that. My relationship with my family is already shit. And I don't want to be different. I want to be normal. I just want to be normal, and I'm scared that I'll never be normal again."

"What would happen if you did have to keep it secret?"

"I would..." Keoghan's voice trailed off. "I don't know."

"Would your relationship get any worse?"

"No."

Soledad offered a small smile. "And do you think being gay isn't normal?"

"I guess it is for some people, but it's not normal for me. I've always only liked men. It's a change, to like a woman."

"You could be bisexual."

Keoghan sat up. "Bisexual? I'm sorry, I never knew much about gay things. I wasn't allowed to know."

Soledad pointed to a book on the geode table. "Open to page 4."

Picking up the book, Keoghan read the cover aloud. "*Queer: The Beginner's Guide to All Things LGBTQ+.*"

She opened to page 4 as instructed, and continued to read. *"Bisexuality: The attraction to two or more genders, often referred to as attraction to both men and women. Bisexual people can have preferences in gender, and potential differences in preference for sexual, romantic, and aesthetic attraction."*

Fear ran through her body. It made sense. She felt like it described her. But she couldn't- she couldn't be even somewhat gay. She couldn't. She just couldn't.

"Does that strike true with you?" Soledad asked gently.

"I think it does," Keoghan whispered. "God, I don't want to be gay. I can't be gay."

"It's important to accept every part of your identity, but if you aren't ready... it's okay to not be ready, Keoghan. It really is okay." Tears began to prick at Keoghan's eyes, threatening to ruin her makeup. "I can't be gay."

Soledad shook her head. "Would you like to process this, or would you like me to distract you with a trauma assessment? Distraction is a valid way of managing distress."

"I need to talk about something else, first. What we were going to talk about last time, before I blacked out," Keoghan told her, the memory of William's second near-rape flooding her mind. "I saw William's ghost again. He wanted to rape me in my bathroom and kill me. He kept calling me a bitch."

"I'm so sorry, Keoghan. I would like to affirm for you that you did not deserve any of that, and that you will get better. But I would also like to know how you're feeling about it."

"I'm terrified. I wasn't even asleep that time. I'm scared he's real, he's going to come after me, he's going to take me and kill me and rape me and-" Keoghan's breath came in shallow, rapid gasps. Her heart pounded. Her head spun.

"Breathe with me, Keoghan," she heard Soledad say. "In. Hold. Out."

She did, following Soledad's verbal cues as to how she should breathe. She felt her heart rate slow, her breathing steady. This time, it worked.

"I think we need to do a PTSD assessment," Soledad told her. "It's soon, but the degree of your problems call for one."

Keoghan nodded. "Alright."

"So I have PTSD now," Keoghan told her friends that evening in the dining hall. "Wild."

Iris nodded. "You seem... calm."

"I guess it's comforting to know that I'm not crazy. My brain is just doing its post-traumatic stress thing."

"I felt the same way when I was diagnosed," Chloe added. "It was like a weight came off my shoulders."

"Exactly. And I can manage it with enough time and skills."

Iris reached over and took Keoghan's hand, sending her heart fluttering. "I'm glad you're seeing Soledad. You deserve to heal."

Elizabeth smiled. "I see a different therapist at Soledad's office, and she always speaks highly of her. You not only deserve to heal, you will."

"Thank you. I really appreciate all of you being here for me with this."

"Of course," Iris smiled. "You're our friend. I would go to hell and back to make sure you heal from William's bullshit."

She squeezed her hand, and Keoghan felt at peace. Her friends would protect her. Iris would be with her over break. She *could* be safe with them. She *deserved* to be safe with them. She *would* be safe with them.

"So, Thanksgiving break," Eri said. "Is anyone else going home?"

"Keoghan's coming with me," Iris told the group. "She just doesn't know it yet."

Keoghan had, in fact, forgotten that Thanksgiving was a thing. Her family didn't celebrate.

"I'm going with you for Thanksgiving and Christmas? Won't your family get tired of me?"

"Never. They'll absolutely love you."

Keoghan smiled, but she wondered about Lukas. He had to go home, she knew that much. She wished he had a friend like Iris, someone who could take him away from the horrors of his family.

It would be fine. He was strong. He could survive one more holiday.

10

Keoghan spent much of her free time with Iris and Celena, often studying for some classes they had together. They met in cafes or libraries. She felt herself feel freer, slowly more stable. She began to eat more regularly. She ate more than 1000 calories. Sure, she felt incredibly guilty and wanted to die, but she was doing it. She was saving herself.

"Hey, Kay!" Celena shouted. "Look at this!"

Keoghan was sitting in her floor common room, scrolling on her phone while she waited for her tea to boil in the microwave as she didn't own a kettle.

"Look at what?" she asked, glancing over to the fiery woman. Celena was holding a flyer and shoved it in Keoghan's face.

"There's a battle of the bands tonight!"

Keoghan nodded. "And you want to go?"

"Fuck yeah I do," Celena cried.

"Alright. Who do you want to go with?"

"Eri's going with that fuckass kid Ben," she groaned. "So I guess you, Iris, Chloe, Liv, and me?"

"Sounds good. Come get me from my dorm when it's time," Keoghan smiled. "I have to pick out something to wear..."

When Celena and the entourage of friends arrived at Keoghan's dorm, she had just finished applying her makeup. She stepped out into the hallway and smiled.

"Let's rock this shit," Celena said firmly. "Oh, Kay, Lukas's meeting us there."

"How did you find that out- whatever. Let's go."

They walked to the quad, where the battle would take place, and found a small crowd gathered around a makeshift stage. Two bands were warming up on either side of a microphone.

"I expected more people," Elizabeth commented.

"It's good that there's less, Liza," Chole smiled. "We can get pit views."

A woman stepped up to the microphone with a wide grin. "Welcome to the Third Annual Stanford Battle of the Bands! Damn, that's a mouthful. Tonight we have two bands competing for your hearts and the amazing prize of bragging rights. Please welcome Lucid Lightning and Cobweb Hearts!"

Applause sounded from the miniscule amount of people present.

"Alright," a member from the band Keoghan assumed to be Lucid Lightning said, stepping up to the mic. "We have a special song for one person in the crowd tonight, something to remember us by. It's a cover."

Keoghan looked at the band, one woman seeming familiar to her. She had blonde hair in a sharp bob and wore entirely leather. Something about her reminded Keoghan of someone...

"Cassidy?" she murmured. "Hey, it's Cassidy!"

Cassidy stepped up to her band's mic and smirked into the crowd. "This is for Nick, 'cause I know she don't remember shit. Nick, let's do it again sometime."

"I'd be the last to say I've got problems..."

Keoghan watched in awe as Cassidy purred into the mic, her band creating a sound of heavy rock that Keoghan had never heard before.

"Goddamn, baby, you drink like Hemingway..."

After the song ended, Cassidy walked down the stairs of the stage and to Keoghan.

"Nick, whaddaya say?"

Keoghan laughed. "I... Sure?"

Cassidy kissed her, and then pulled away. "This is the last time, 'kay? I gotta girl I'm lookin' at, but I wanted to kiss ya one more time."

"Alright," Keoghan smiled. "Thanks, Cassidy."

"No prob, hun."

The crowd cheered as she kissed her one more time.

As Cassidy walked away, Keoghan looked to Iris. The woman was staring with her eyebrows knit together and her teeth clenched.

"Hey, it's fine, Iris," Celena said quickly. "Keoghan's allowed to have fun."

Iris nodded quickly. "I know. I know."

"Want to stay for the other band?"

"Yeah, of course. Keoghan, you good?"

"Of course," Keoghan laughed. "I'm great."

The second band did their soundcheck, and one of the members stepped up to the mic.

"We're Cobweb Hearts, and we're also doing a cover... but we won't kiss the audience, even though the cover is also a Girl in Red song."

They returned to their seat at the drums, and the crowd cheered.

"You let the wrong people love you, but you don't see that, do you?"

Iris smiled. "I know this song."

"You stupid bitch, can't you see? The perfect one for you is me..."

Keoghan nodded along and looked over at her friends.

Iris was staring directly at her.

Thanksgiving break arrived quicker than Keoghan could ever have imagined. She had been busy with classwork, as the semester was beginning to draw to a close. Additionally, her friends had kept her running all around campus and town to spend time with them. She and Iris had several more study "dates", and Iris briefed her on her family. Finally, the two women piled their suitcases and selves into Iris's car and drove to Portland.

"I'm so nervous," Keoghan laughed, raking her hands through her hair. "What if I'm not the right person for them?"

Iris smiled and shook her head. "Trust me, you'll be fine. They accept me, so they'll totally accept you."

"Accept you for what? You seem like the perfect daughter."

"I..." Iris's voice trailed off, and Keoghan watched her chest rise and fall as she took deep breaths. "I haven't told anyone here, but... I'm trans. I was born a guy and went onto puberty blockers pretty early. I started estrogen as soon as I could."

Keoghan nodded slowly. "Wow."

"I'm sorry. I hope you don't see me any differently, I know it's big, but..."

"Iris. You're still my close friend. You're still Iris. I don't see you as anyone except that."

"Yeah. Close friend."

They fell into silence until the radio began to turn into static.

"Can I play music?" Keoghan asked.

Iris nodded. "Yeah, of course. My phone isn't connected right now, anyway."

Keoghan paired her phone to the car and began to play a song from one of her guilty pleasure movies, *Winter Spring Summer or Fall*. She loved the innocent, first love of the film and the way everything worked out like it had to. Whenever she watched it, she hoped something like it would come for her.

"Spending all our money on all our friends' shows, tell me that this drink's on you, 'cause I don't think my card will go through..."

Iris smiled as she heard the lyrics. "Winter Spring Summer or Fall?"

Keoghan's eyes bulged out of her head. "You know that movie?"

"Dude, I love that movie! Have you seen *My Old Ass*?"

"Yes!"

"I'm a tragic queer, but I love Percy Hynes White."

Keoghan laughed softly. "Crazy."

"Missing my lover on a night out, feeling lonely when the lights go out, meet me where I'm at..."

"Iris?" Keoghan asked. "Can I tell you something?"

Iris nodded. "Yeah. Anything."

"I... I might be bisexual. I don't know. It's bad. I just-"

"I accept you, Keoghan. And trust me, I know what your queer awakening terror is like."

Keoghan smiled. "Thank you."

"Do you want to talk through it? I'm assuming you already did with Soledad, but if you want my ears..."

"That would be great, actually."

Iris took one hand off of the wheel to squeeze Keoghan's. "Whenever you're ready."

"I guess... I met this girl. And I really liked her. And she would do things that would make my heart feel so happy and light and good. And I didn't want to be gay, not at all, not with my family. But I'm accepting it now. Bisexuality."

"Do I know this girl?"

Keoghan blanched. Fuck. "Uh, yes."

"I won't make you tell me who it is. Just know that, whenever you're ready, I'm here to listen and help," Iris told her.

"Meet me where I'm at, meet me where I'm at, meet me where I'm at..."

The rest of the car ride passed with chatter and music as Keoghan got to know Iris one-on-one. When they arrived at Iris's parents' house, she knew for sure: she liked Iris. A lot.

Iris unlocked the door, and her parents rushed up to her.

"Baobao, welcome home!" her mother cried. "And your friend is here with you!"

"Mama, this is Keoghan," Iris told her. "Keoghan, this is-"

Iris's mother smiled widely. "Keoghan! What a beautiful name. My name is Meng Xin."

"Do you want her English name?" Iris asked Keoghan, who shook her head.

"Meng Xin. I can pronounce that," Keoghan responded.

"Oh, so polite!" Meng Xin laughed. "Keoghan, this is my husband, Qiu."

"Nice to meet you both. Thank you for letting me stay with you."

"Of course! Oh, I'm so happy that my little girl has a close friend. I always knew college would make her come out of her shell," Meng Xin told her. "Now, we have dinner ready. I made soup dumplings!"

Iris smiled widely. "Really? Thank you, Mama."

"Yes, of course! Take off your shoes and come eat!"

Keoghan removed her shoes and followed Iris, Meng Xin, and Qiu to the dining room. Soup dumplings. Her stomach growled quietly, and for the first time that she could remember, she wanted to honor it. The house was covered in artwork and vases, and it was obvious some of the art was Iris's. She had only known the family for a few minutes, but she already felt at home. Maybe this was what family could (and should) be.

The Song family's guest room was upstairs next to Iris's room, and they shared a bathroom. Keoghan sat at Iris's desk facing the window as the other woman changed in the bathroom, though she occasionally spun around to look at Iris's decorations. Her deep blue walls were covered in space posters and the occasional movie poster, and her ceiling had glow-in-the-dark stars. There was a planet-shaped rug next to the desk, which was under a lofted bed.

"You really like space, huh?" Keoghan asked when Iris stepped back into the room.

"Yeah," Iris smiled. "I would have become an astronomer if anyone else could take over the tech company."

"Why didn't you double-major?"

"I don't know, honestly. I think I'm going to stick with Business, though."

Keoghan nodded. "Fair. We should go look at stars sometime."

"Yeah," Iris nodded. "Your eyes are kind of like stars. They stand out, 'cause they're so light green."

A blush rose on Keoghan's face. "You like them?"

"A lot!"

"I've always hated my eyes."

"They're pretty. So are you. I hope you know that."

Keoghan swore she was as red as blood. "Thank you. You're really pretty, as well. Like, *really* pretty."

Iris smiled and sat down on a beanbag next to Keoghan. "I'm so glad you're here. My family's never met anybody I know before because, well... I didn't really talk to people before college. I felt like everyone only saw me as transgender, not as a person. That's why I hid it when I went to Stanford."

"You're a person first, transgender second," Keoghan told her. "Just like I'm learning to accept that I'm a person first and... bisexual... second."

"We'll learn to accept it together. One day at a time."

11

The next day, Keoghan and Iris went to Powell's City of Books. Iris had told her about it on the drive, and it lived up to Keoghan's expectations. The bookshop took up an entire city block and was four stories tall.

"This is a mindfuck," Keoghan whispered to Iris as they walked through the shop. "There's so many *books!*"

Iris laughed quietly and nodded. "I know, right? Let me show you my favorite part."

She took Keoghan's hand in hers and led her to a corridor filled with branches of bookshelves. Keoghan held her hand tightly, and, despite herself, wished that Iris would never let go.

Fuck, she really was gay.

That was even more of a mindfuck than the store.

"Look at this," Iris told her.

Keoghan followed Iris's gaze. The store looked like a magic portal of books from the angle they were at, shelves in every corner of her vision.

"It's beautiful," Keoghan murmured. "I could stay here forever."

"We have a whole day ahead of us. Let's get lost and look at books."

Not letting go of Iris's hand, Keoghan pulled her through the shelves and gazed at the different titles. Eventually, she saw one that jumped her memory back to William, the last thing she wanted to think of when she was with Iris.

But I Asked For It: Sexual Assault Survivors' Stories.

Iris followed her glance to the book and squeezed her hand.

"Do you want to buy it, or shove it deep into the shelf?" she asked.

Keoghan leaned her head on Iris's shoulder and sighed. "I don't know. I just... I'm sorry for ruining this trip."

"Keoghan," Iris told her, looking her in the eye and cupping her cheek with her free hand. "You're not ruining anything. You have trauma. Fuck, you have PTSD. You're allowed to have responses to things that trigger you."

Tears began to prick at Keoghan's eyes, and she leaned forward, pressing her forehead against Iris's. "Thank you. I... I really appreciate you."

"Of course. I'm always here."

They stood in between the shelves, foreheads pressed together, for what felt like an eternity. Keoghan didn't want to move away, not ever. She just wanted to have Iris, just like this, until she, too, got torn away from her.

After they left Powell's Books, Keoghan and Iris walked downtown to go to a coffee shop. When they entered, Keoghan froze. The barista had mousy brown hair and deep hazel eyes, and the angular structure of his cheeks looked exactly like William's.

Fuck.

Fuck.

Fuck fuck fuck fuck fuck.

Keoghan

Couldn't

Think

Or

Move

Or

Speak

She

Just

Felt

The

World

Collapse.

"I'm coming for you, almond milk bitch. You're going to be so good for me."

"Keoghan!"

Keoghan's brain was spinning, but slowly the world pieced itself back together. Iris was holding her close to her chest, rubbing circles on her back.

"Keoghan, are you alright?"

"William..." Keoghan breathed. "He's coming for me."

"No, he's not. You're with me. You're safe. That barista is not William, I promise."

"I need... I can't... Go..."

Iris nodded and took her hand, helping her walk. "Let's go. We'll find a different coffee shop."

Keoghan walked out of the building on weak legs, leaning heavily on Iris for support. Once they crossed the threshold, she felt William's icy grip on her heart release slowly.

"Do you need to go home?" Iris asked. "We can."

"No," Keoghan whispered. "I ruined this day already. I don't want to make it worse."

"You didn't ruin the day. Like I said in Powell's, you're still healing. I'm here for all of you, not just the brave face I know you put on."

Keoghan sighed. "I'm sorry."

"Don't be. Let's go home, and I'll make you tea," Iris told her.

"Alright."

Once they arrived at Iris's house, the two women headed for the kitchen, where Keoghan sat at the island while Iris made tea.

"Jasmine, yuzu, or pomegranate?" Iris asked.

"Pomegranate, please."

As the tea steeped, Iris sat next to her and leaned her head on Keoghan's shoulder.

"I'm glad you came here."

Keoghan closed her eyes and exhaled. She was safe. Iris was with her.

The two women spent the rest of the day drinking tea and perusing the bookshelves in the Song house. Keoghan was relaxed, moreso than she had been in a long time, in no small part thanks to Iris.

Maybe Thanksgiving break wasn't that bad of a time.

12

Thanksgiving. Keoghan never knew what to do with that holiday, as her family refused to celebrate. She wished Lukas were with her instead of at his parents' house; she was having such a good time and he was alone with his parents' strangling influence.

In the morning of the holiday, Iris took her to the store to buy a last-minute seasoning kit. The drive was short, the radio crooned the first Christmas song of the season. As they stood in the checkout line, Keoghan heard her phone chime. It was a text from her mother.

Your cousin was found dead in his room. He hanged himself. You will be expected to attend his funeral.

The world seemed like it stood still, but at the same time was rapidly turning upside down.

No.

Not Lukas.

Not Lukas.

Instead of pricking at her eyes as they normally did, the tears assaulted Keoghan's face. How embarrassing, to cry in a Kroger, but she didn't care. Lukas was dead.

Lukas killed himself.

Lukas killed himself because she wasn't there to save him.

"Keoghan?" Iris asked. "What happened? Is it William?"

"Lukas..." Keoghan wailed. "Lukas is dead."

Iris's eyes widened. "What?"

"Lukas killed himself."

"No. *What?*"

"It's all my fault," Keoghan sobbed. "I didn't spend Thanksgiving with him. He was alone. He was with his fuckass family. I killed my own cousin. Iris, he's *gone*. He's *gone*. I'm never going to see him again. He's *gone*."

Iris wrapped Keoghan in her arms and held her as sobs racked her body. "You didn't kill him. I promise. He wouldn't want you to blame yourself."

"He's gone..."

"I know. I know. I'm so sorry, Keoghan."

"What am I supposed to do now?"

ACT TWO:
THORNS

13

LUKAS'S INTERLUDE

Lukas Lancaster was not normal. That much he had known since his first breath of consciousness. He also knew that his purpose in life was to be another link in his family's horrid chain, and the only way to break it would be to die.

So, he resolved to die.

The only reason he didn't do it sooner was Keoghan.

Keoghan, Keo, his Jester. She stood by him when nobody else did, kept him sane when his family tried their hardest to drive him to the brink of madness.

He knew he wouldn't regret death, but he would regret leaving her behind.

When the time came, he sent a letter to the address she had told him she would be at, using his father's emergency credit card to pay for expedited shipping. He unlocked a trunk at the foot of his bed and felt the rope he had hidden there in his hands.

It felt like freedom.

Bittersweet freedom.

14

ICE HAVEN

"I swear to God, Keo, you're going to kill me!" Lukas laughed, out of breath as he jogged to catch up to his cousin. "It's fucking fifteen degrees, not to mention midnight, and we're going for a run?"

Keoghan, his best friend and only real family, turned to run backward and smirked at him. "You know that your rink is open twenty-four-seven."

"Is that why you have that mysterious bag slung over your shoulder?"

A blue and white canvas bag was, in fact, hanging from Keoghan's bony shoulder. Lukas tried to ignore her thinning frame and focused on the tote bag.

"If you don't hurry up, I'll get to Ice Haven before you and steal your skates from the very bag I carry," Keoghan teased.

Ice Haven was the name of the ice rink Lukas skated at and his second- or maybe first- home. Keoghan often accompanied him there, and it was usually at unpopular hours. Nobody could know that Lukas Lancaster liked figure skating. Especially not anyone who could tell his parents.

Lukas picked up his pace and grazed the bag with his fingers as he maneuvered past Keoghan. He had the advantage in this town-Keoghan was a visitor. Whereas both of their families were in upstate

New York, they lived in separate cities. Still, she had walked or run the route to Ice Haven enough to mitigate the chances of getting lost.

"I'll buy you a drink at the Ice if you can beat me," Lukas challenged with a smile. "And I won't make you play the song on your phone."

Keoghan nodded and saluted him. "You're on. I'm going to set you back a coffee."

The two began to sprint faster, exerting as much energy as they could to boost their momentum. Both knew that in the long run, it was better to save yourself, but neither cared. Ice Haven was only a few minutes away from the Lancaster family home anyway.

As he ran, Lukas began to time the thuds of his feet hitting the ground with his favorite song to skate to. It was childish, but he had been building a routine inspired by a show he had watched with Keoghan when they were nine, the very same show that had inspired him to skate.

"*Can you feel my heartbeat?*" he mumbled under his breath. "*Tired of feeling never enough...*"

Keoghan's strained laugh floated over to him. "Yuri on fucking Ice never left your brain, did it?"

"Hey, I know you do that with your weird interests, too," Lukas argued. "Hello Kitty, perchance?"

Keoghan groaned and flipped him off.

"And," Lukas continued, "it's reasonable that it never left my brain. I mean, Yuri and Viktor... that's just about as close to a dream as it gets."

"You and only you," Keoghan smiled. She slowed down and leaned against the railing of a bridge they were crossing, breathing heavily.

Lukas placed a hand on her shoulder and took the bag off of it. "Are you alright?"

"Just, you know, lightheaded. It's fine. I think I haven't had enough water."

"And food?" Lukas asked, crossing his arms.

"Come on, Reg, don't start this now. Like I said, it's fine," Keoghan snapped. "Let's keep going."

Lukas nodded, but made a point of walking instead of running. He was worried about his cousin; she was deteriorating in front of him and there was nothing he could do. No matter how much he reminded her to eat, begged her, yelled at her, she stood steadfast in her self-destruction. Keoghan stared into the neighborhood as they approached Ice Haven, and Lukas wondered if she was ignoring him.

Once the pair arrived at the rink, Lukas pulled the door open for his cousin and reveled in the indoor air washing over him. Ice Haven was his safe place.

Keoghan took a seat at a bench next to the rink, seeming more unsteady than usual. Lukas pulled his skates out of the tote bag and put them on. It was fine. She wouldn't want his help. He stepped onto the ice.

After a few warm-up laps, he noticed that Keoghan wasn't watching him anymore. She must have been laying down.

"Keo, can you play the music? My phone should be next to you," he called.

No response.

"Keo?"

Skating over to the edge of the ice, Lukas saw his cousin splayed out on the ground, the rise and fall of her chest slow and her usually tan face appearing ashen.

Fuck.

He moved to the rink exit as fast as he could, pulling off his skates and running over to her. Placing a hand on her chest, he felt a weak heartbeat.

Fuck, fuck, fuck, fuck, fuck.

There must have been someone working. Had they not seen her? Did they think she was sleeping? Lukas ran to the skate rental window and banged on the wooden counter.

"Help, we need someone to- someone, help!" he cried. Footsteps sounded, but they were taking too long. Everything was taking too long. Keoghan might be dead. She was dying. Fuck. Fuck. Fuck. His face was hot. His limbs were hot. He couldn't feel anything except heat, except himself hyperventilating, except his thoughts hammering at his skull.

"What do you need, kid?" a young man drawled. "We have a first-aid kit over there-"

"My cousin is fucking dying," Lukas screamed. "She is- she is passed out on the floor and I can barely feel her heartbeat and- holy fucking shit- fuck, fuck, fuck..."

The man's eyes widened, and he walked away from the window. A few seconds later, he was kneeling on the floor next to Keoghan.

"Have you called 911?"

"No, I..." Lukas's voice trailed off. "Fuck..."

"Easy. It's okay to be stressed out. Where's your phone?" the man asked.

Lukas picked his phone up off of the bench and pressed the Emergency Call button. He heard himself talk to the operator, heard her tell him that an ambulance would be at Ice Haven as soon as they could be, heard her ask him to remain on the phone, heard the man tell him that everything would be okay.

For all the hearing he was doing, he certainly didn't comprehend anything.

He forgot his skates at Ice Haven when the ambulance came.

As far as he knew, they were still there. Maybe they were given to someone else.

He never went back.

15

LUKAS AND CASSIDY

Lukas met Cassidy Ames on his first day at Stanford in his English class. She had sat next to him as he applied chapstick that Keoghan forced him to use.

"Puttin' on your lipstick, gay boy?" she asked with a wide smile.

Lukas blanched and capped the chapstick. "I'm- I'm not-"

"Kiddin', hun. My name's Cassidy, and I'm gonna be your friend. Now, are ya sure you're not gay? You've got the... the vibes," she told him, making a rainbow with her hands.

"I'm not..." Lukas clenched his teeth together. "...out to anyone except my cousin."

Cassidy nodded. "It's okay, gay boy. We all have to start somewhere."

 "Are you...?" Lukas asked quietly.

"Hell yeah. I'm a womankisser through and through."

"You should meet my cousin," Lukas told her, words pouring out of his mouth. "She's a great person, and I think you could help her a bit."

"Is she gay?" Cassidy asked, leaning back in her chair and stretching her arms out in front of her. "And if she is, is she pretty?"

Lukas shook his head. What was he doing? Keoghan wouldn't like Cassidy... would she? Still, he wanted her to have a friend after he- *if* he didn't survive his own mind.

"She's not gay, I don't think. But you should meet her. She's cool."
Cassidy nodded. "Alright. Let's meet your cousin."

LUKAS'S LETTER

Dear Keo,

By the time you read this, I'll be gone. I know that's a generic opener, but I didn't know what else to say. How do you tell your best friend, your only family, that you're at the end of your rope?

I have nothing for me except for you. I can't hide myself anymore. I can't go into politics. I can't do anything.

I can't live anymore.

Keo, I love you. So, so much. And I never want you to think you're responsible. I have been thinking about this since I was six years old. There's nothing you could have done to save me.

Live on, Keo.

Live for me.

I love you.

Lukas.

THIRTEEN

Keoghan lived in a haze. She sat through Thanksgiving and drove to Stanford with Iris the next day. She scheduled an emergency session with Soledad. She slept. She stopped eating again. She lost more weight. Nothing helped.

The funeral came. Lukas was given an open casket, and Keoghan stared at him for a long while. The rope bruises around his neck screamed to her that it was all her fault. His closed eyes shouted that she should have saved him.

"The doctors gave you until the end of the night, but not 'til daylight," she sang quietly. *"Time passes slower in the flicker of the hospital light, I pray the race is worth the fight..."*

She reached into the casket and brushed her fingers against his. Cold. Icy cold. As she lifted his limp hand, she saw something she had never noticed. His button-down's sleeves slid up, and she saw red lines peek out from underneath them. Waves of pain crashed over her as she slowly lifted the sleeve further to see them marring all of his lower arm and wrist. He had never told her. She had never noticed. She had never questioned why he wore long sleeves in the summer.

Why hadn't she noticed?

She was such a bad person.

She was a horrible person.

Lukas deserved a better cousin than her.

"Tell me all the time not to worry," she murmured. *"And think of all the time I'll have with you..."*

Keoghan fought back tears as she rolled his sleeve back down, lifting his hand to her forehead.

"I love you, Reg," she whispered. "And I'm so fucking sorry."

The lights flickered, and William appeared behind her.

"It's all your fault, almond milk bitch. Lukas and I are two sides of the same coin. We both committed suicide because of you."

"Take his name out of your mouth," Keoghan spat.

"Lukas. Lukas, Lukas, Lukas," William sang, prancing closer to the casket. *"What has she done to you?"*

He traced his finger across Lukas's hollow cheek. Keoghan felt her anger spike, her fists ball.

"Don't fucking touch him. He's not your toy."

"He may not be, but you are. I will have you at my mercy, Keoghan. I will have you exactly how I want you: good for me."

"Fuck. You."

"Gladly," William chuckled, appearing in front of Keoghan in a flash. *"I can only imagine how you'll feel-"*

Keoghan slapped him across his face, and he shattered. Breathing heavily, she felt herself return to reality, where she lay draped over Lukas's casket.

When would it end?

"Lukas Lancaster was a brilliant man set on improving our country."

He never wanted to be a politician.

"He was loved by his parents and their closest family, his aunt, uncle, and cousin."

Keoghan was the only one that he ever thought loved him.

"Hear a few words from his mother, Alexis Lancaster."

Lukas never spoke of his mother. From the interactions Keoghan had with her, she saw her as quiet, yet stern. When she stepped up to the podium, Alexis had tears in her eyes, though she seemed to swallow them down.

"Hello, everybody. Thank you for coming."

A silence.

"Lukas was everything to me. I know we didn't speak often, he was always so busy, but he was my entire heart. I don't want to keep you long. I don't want to bore you with stories from his childhood. I just want to tell everyone, all of you in this crowd: someone out there loves you more than you think they do. And they never, *never* want you to be taken from them."

Keoghan felt tears coming to her own eyes once again. She wondered if Lukas knew that his mother loved him. Did she show it? Or was she so afraid of his father that she couldn't show it? Would she have been able to save him?

Could anyone have saved him? Or was he so beyond gone that any light would have been filtered out before it reached him?

"Keoghan?" Alexis asked gently, staring down at her. "Would you like to say something? He said you two had been closer over the last several months."

Nodding, Keoghan blinked her tears away and took Alexis's place. "Hi. I'm, uh, I'm Keoghan Winchester. Lukas's cousin and, since we both began attending Stanford University, his best friend. And he was mine."

"Lukas was the only man I could trust after something happened to me early in the semester. He stood by my side. He comforted me. He made me feel safe and seen. And there was something I had to tell him, something I couldn't tell him before he died."

Keoghan was bisexual. Lukas would never get to know. He died thinking he was alone in the world of being queer, but he was far from it. Keoghan was there with him all along, even though neither of them knew.

"I just remember... Lukas was the best person I knew. And I miss him so much. Reg, if you're listening, I hope you're happy. I hope you're wherever the good people go, and that you find someone to spend your time with. I hope you're with all the cute cats and all the indie music I know you like. I love you. And thank you, thank you so much for being in my life."

She stepped down from the podium and walked back to her seat, wringing her hands. Lukas was never coming back.

He

Wasn't

Coming

Back.

And she was destroying her life and her health, giving into every thought her mind had about her body.

That wasn't fair to Lukas. It wasn't fair to herself. It wasn't fair to her friends.

She would do something. As soon as she got back, she would do something to save herself.

16

When Keoghan returned to California, Iris met her at the airport.

"Hey, Keoghan," she greeted softly. "How was... everything?"

Keoghan shook her head and dropped it onto Iris's shoulder. "I'm so fucking tired. And I can't believe that Lukas..."

Iris wrapped her arms around her. "I know. I know, Keoghan. It's so hard."

"I just want him back."

"Careful what you wish for, almond milk bitch."

Keoghan ignored William. She didn't have the capacity to deal with him anymore.

"Let's get home," Iris told her. "I think you should get some sleep."

"Iris?" Keoghan whispered as they walked to the car. "I have to tell you something."

"Anything," Iris smiled.

"I think I need help. I... I have an eating disorder, and... I need help. Lukas's passing made me realize that."

Iris nodded. "We'll get you help. I promise."

Eri welcomed Keoghan into their room with a tight hug. "I'm so sorry, Keoghan."

Keoghan nodded against them. "Thank you."

"He came over here all the time, wanting to talk to you. Sometimes he waited for you to come back, other times he had to go to class. He really loved you."

"I loved him too," Keoghan sniffed. "He was my best friend."

Eri smiled gently. "He's never really gone. He's always with you in spirit."

"So am I. Lukas and I, we're gonna kill you for what you did to us."

"William, leave me alone. Lukas isn't going to kill me," Keoghan cried. Eri held them tightly again.

"Leave her the fuck alone, you dickhead. Lukas loved her more than your fucked-up self ever could."

William appeared behind Eri and grinned manically, waving at Keoghan.

"I'll see you tonight, almond milk bitch."

Keoghan slumped against Eri and held them close. "I feel like I'm cursed. Everyone around me keeps dying."

"I won't. I have no intention of dying," Eri told her. "You'll have me for as long as you need me."

The next day, Keoghan went to see Soledad. She lay on the floor and stared at the ceiling, which had recently been draped with sheer pink fabric. Her hands were clasped together, and she did not speak.

"You just returned from Lukas's funeral," Soledad began. "Did you give a eulogy?"

Keoghan nodded. "Yes."

"How was that experience?"

"It was..." Keoghan's voice trailed off. "I don't know. His mother gave one first, and that was hard to follow."

"I'd imagine. How are you feeling? Any guilt, shame, fear..." Soledad asked.

"All of it? And William has been coming back more often. He keeps telling me that he's going to kill me, and that Lukas is going to help him."

"Do you think Lukas would help him?"

"Absolutely not."

"I want you to know that this William is not real," Soledad told her. "He is dead, and regardless of your personal beliefs in ghosts, this sounds like a trauma-induced hallucination. You are safe. He cannot hurt you anymore."

"Thank you. I just have to try to remember that," Keoghan sighed.

"It will come in time. I'd like to work on another distress tolerance skill today to help you through this time..."

Keoghan stood outside of her dorm, leaning against a wall with a white Monster in her hand.

"Hey, Lukas," she whispered to nobody. "I got one of these for you. I remember how you used to sneak them into school and drink them in the bathrooms."

A cold wind blew through her hair, and she felt alertness spread in her body. Maybe it was the energy drink, or maybe it was the feeling of being watched. She looked around and saw nobody.

Then, a woman stepped out of the shadows.

Cassidy.

"Hey, Nick," she greeted, a strained smile on her face. "How're you doin' with... y'know?"

Keoghan nodded slowly and bit her lip. "Just surviving. How about you? I know you were friends with... with Lukas."

Cassidy shrugged. "We weren't all too close, but I miss that son of a bitch so bad. My precious gay boy, gone."

"Yeah," Keoghan murmured. "Cassidy?"

"M-hmm?"

"My name's not actually Nick."

Cassidy's smile became more genuine, and she chuckled gently. "Oh, I know. Your name's Keoghan Winchester."

Keoghan's eyes widened. "Did Lukas tell you that?"

"He did. I just let you call yourself Nick 'cause, well, you seemed to like it." She reached into her purse, a small black bag that Keoghan couldn't imagine held much of anything, and pulled out a cigarette. "Want one, hun?"

"Uh..." Keoghan didn't know. She didn't necessarily want to smoke, but she wanted a distraction. "Sure."

Cassidy handed her one and lit them both with a sparkly pink lighter. "Losin' someone sucks, don't it?"

"Yeah," Keoghan sighed, taking a long draw from the cigarette and breaking into a coughing fit.

"Easy," Cassidy laughed. "The first couple times you do it, it's bad, but it'll get less cough-y."

"It tastes really bad."

"Price of fun, hun. You don't have to do it again if you hate it."

Keoghan nodded. "I think this once is enough for me. I'm not really into... y'know... drugs... unless I really need something."

"You're a crisis user," Cassidy said sagely. "I get that. We all start there. Just watch yourself, 'kay? I don't want you in crisis, on the streets, shooting up or something."

"Oh, God, no," Keoghan grimaced. "That sounds like hell."

"Hell indeed. Look, hun, I gotta go. I'll see you 'round campus?"

"Yeah. See you around."

As Cassidy walked away, Keoghan took one last hit of the cigarette and coughed violently. She extinguished it and dropped it in a trash can, then walking up the stairs to her dorm. It hadn't occurred to her that Lukas's death could affect anyone other than his family. Seeing Cassidy mourning rekindled the wildfire of grief taking over her body. Lukas had been important to others. He had been a friend. And now... now he was gone.

Elizabeth and Chloe knocked on Keoghan's door the next morning, carrying a bouquet of white roses.

"Keoghan!" Chloe cried as soon as Keoghan opened the door. "Jesus fuck, I missed you. I heard about Lukas. I'm so fucking sorry."

Elizabeth smiled gently and handed her the flowers. "You are so strong. How are you?"

"I-" Keoghan was cut off as a flurry of red hair burst through the other two women.

"KAY!" Celena shouted, wrapping Keoghan in a hug. "Oh my God, Kay... Are you okay?"

Keoghan laughed and hugged her back, making sure to place the flowers on the closest surface first. "I will be. Thank you for the loud greeting, I'm sure my floormates will love this."

"Anytime. Liv, Chloe, you're coming with us to go to breakfast. I don't care if you've eaten, I'll get you a drink."

Elizabeth chuckled and stepped out of the doorframe. "Lead the way, Celena."

As they walked, Celena chattered to Keoghan about the classes she had missed and how she and Iris had been taking notes for her. Keoghan thanked her many times. Eventually, they arrived at the dining room and Celena turned the conversation to Keoghan's life.

"Did that bitchass guy come back? Do I need to punch through his horrible face?"

"He did. Several times, actually," Keoghan sighed. "But there's not much you can do, and if you tried to punch him you might end up punching me. I appreciate it, though. I'll punch him for you."

"If he comes back."

"Oh, he will come back."

"You don't say, almond milk bitch."

"Can't you come up with a new nickname?" Keoghan groaned. "It's getting old."

"How about my dearest slut?"

"Don't call me a slut."

"I'm only speaking the truth."

Keoghan whirled around and smiled grimly. "Oh, trust me, you aren't." She threw a punch directly in his face, and he shattered.

"Kay..." Celena called, waving a hand in front of Keoghan's face. "Did you get him?"

Keoghan nodded and smiled. "I sure as hell did."

17

Keoghan sat at her desk later in the day, twirling a pen in her hand. She wanted to do something, anything other than sitting around in her own sorrow and procrastinating classwork.

Pulling out her phone, she googled *'activities to do for grief'*. It had been something that Soledad suggested in their previous session. She scrolled through the webpages, finding nothing, until she saw one suggestion that resonated with her.

"Write a letter to the person you lost and burn it, imagining the ashes traveling to wherever you believe they would be."

She grabbed a pad of paper and clicked open her pen, putting it to the paper. What should she write? Should she make it a dump of her emotions? No. She didn't want to burden Lukas's soul. A joke? He wouldn't appreciate that.

Dear Lukas, she wrote.

I don't know what to write here. Honest, maybe a little bit too much? She debated scratching it out, but suddenly felt overcome with emotion and words.

I miss you. It hasn't been that long, but I miss you so much. You were closer to me than an ordinary family member; my best friend. I hope you're doing well, wherever you are, and...

Tears began to trickle down her cheeks, wetting the paper.

I hope you're happy now. I hope you get to live how you never could, be who you never could. I love you, and I will until our kingdom collapses. Reg and the Jester forever.

Love,

Keo, your court maniac.

Keoghan pressed the letter close to her chest and wiped her eyes. It was time to burn it. She walked into the courtyard of her residence hall and sighed. No lighter. Looking around, she saw a man in the corner, smoking.

"Excuse me," she began, walking over to him, "can I borrow your lighter?"

The man looked up, and Keoghan saw William's image. She jumped backwards, and it disappeared, leaving a confused look on the man's real face.

He extended his lighter. "...sure?"

"Great. Thanks," she rushed, grabbing the lighter and lighting the paper on every corner, then handing it back to him. The paper was eaten by the flame faster than she could imagine Lukas in whatever afterlife existed, and she dropped it just as it would have burned her hand. It extinguished on the way down, leaving one phrase staring up at her.

Reg and the Jester forever.

"Forever," Keoghan murmured, picking up the paper and ripping it in half. She ascended the stairs back to her dorm and threw it out the hallway window, watching the two scraps fly in the wind.

Lukas was gone.

Keoghan lost her sense of time.

Soledad gave Keoghan a self-help book for eating disorders somewhere along the way. She read it, and tried to apply the skills.

It only helped if she wanted it to.

A few days later, a knock sounded on Keoghan's door. She opened it, and there stood Iris, holding a flyer.

"Okay," Iris began as soon as the door was open, "I know this sounds really stupid, but... I wanted to show it to you."

She handed Keoghan the flyer before Keoghan could even speak.

"Eating Disorder Support Group," Keoghan read aloud. "It's not stupid, I just don't know if it's my thing."

Iris smiled gently. "I... You should go. Just once. Try it?"

Keoghan nodded. She didn't want to go. She didn't want to see people who were sicker than her, smaller than her, better than her.

But it was Iris who had asked.

"Alright. I'll go."

A few days later, the support group meeting came. Keoghan rode her bike to the location and locked it outside the building, which appeared to be a repurposed greenhouse. As she entered, the smell of roses overwhelmed her.

"We have a new face, then!" a chipper woman smiled as soon as Keoghan sat on an available chair. "Welcome!"

Keoghan grimaced and nodded. "Yeah. Hi."

One woman, a small blonde with her thin hair in a ponytail, crossed her arms. "You're so skinny. What's your BMI?"

"Cat, we don't ask those questions here," the chipper woman reprimanded. "I know you're new, but you should know the ground rules-"

"I'm sorry about her," a man sighed, shaking his head. "I'm Alec. Recovering bulimic, if you care to know. I'm a veteran of this group, been coming since I moved here."

"It's alright. I'm, uh... I'm Nick," Keoghan told him.

"Nice to meet you, Nick. Now spill. What's your poison?"

"Posion?"

Alec shrugged. "You know. Starve? Purge? I know you don't binge, you lucky girl, but there's a reason you're here."

Keoghan pursed her lips. "Well, I... I need to go, actually. Yeah. I forgot I had to go to a doctor's appointment, and I biked here, so..."

She got up and sped out of the room, leaving the small group behind.

There was a reason she hated eating disorder treatment, even if not clinical.

Keoghan knocked on Iris's door as soon as she returned to campus.

"You're back early," Iris greeted. "Not your thing?"

"Absolutely not," Keoghan exhaled.

"Come in. We can talk about it, if you want."

Keoghan plopped down on Iris's chair and sighed. "The first second I was there, some girl asked me about my BMI, and then some guy started interrogating me. I don't think I'll be going back."

"Damn." Iris shook her head. "I'm sorry. I was hoping it would be good."

"I think... I think I'll try to do something on my own," Keoghan half-lied. She wasn't sure if she wanted to do anything anymore, but she owed it to Iris. She owed it to Lukas.

Iris smiled. "I'm glad."

Goal achieved.

Keoghan sat in her floor's common area, white Monster in hand. In the time since Lukas's death, she had found herself drinking more and more of them, pouring a little out for him every time. She never told anyone about her coping mechanism.

That day, something inside her told her to post her drink on her Instagram story. She didn't know why, but she snapped a picture.

A toast to the fallen, she wrote.

Post.

Almost immediately, her friends began to like the story. She smiled. It felt good to get attention online, even if it was for something as silly as a drink. The notifications stopped, and she set her phone down.

Then, one final ping sounded. Keoghan checked her Instagram and let out a small gasp.

alexis.lancaster has liked your story.

alexis.lancaster has sent you a message.

Keoghan's blood ran cold. Lukas's mother. What was she going to say? Keoghan debated opening the message, navigating to and away from the message tab of the app.

Finally, she clicked on it.

alexis.lancaster: *Thank you.*

Confusion clouded Keoghan's mind. What did she mean? Did she know that Keoghan was drinking the energy drink for Lukas?

keothejester: *For what?*

Her phone buzzed again instantly.

alexis.lancaster: *I know Lukas used to sneak those things into school. You're giving him the remembrance he would have liked.*

Keoghan's eyes began to water, and she leaned her head on her hand. She never knew Alexis felt anything other than neutrality toward her son. To read her message felt like a stab to the gut. Still, Keoghan knew that the stab was good. She needed to feel it. Maybe her picture gave Alexis the same reaction.

keothejester: *It's the least I could do.*

Finals week. Keoghan had been dreading it since Thanksgiving, and it had arrived. None of her classes had extraordinarily difficult finals, but she still felt nervous going into her classes. The ever-present threat of William followed her throughout her days, and the equally present depression after losing Lukas clouded her mind, despite her letter. *Reg and the Jester forever.* Her Monster consumption skyrocketed.

When she walked into her first class final of the day, one where Iris and Celena awaited her, she could practically hear Lukas in her mind.

"You're going to do great, Keo. I promise. Don't listen to William. He's just trying to get you weak, and you are not weak. His voice will go away. You will get through this."

Keoghan took a deep breath and sat down. "You're right. Thank you, Reg. I will get through this."

Celena tapped on her shoulder. "You're getting that trance thing again, but you don't look like it's hurting you. Are you okay?"

Keoghan nodded. "It's Lukas. He's with me now."

"Tell him to tell William to back the fuck off."

"Trust me, I will do my best to do that," Lukas laughed.

"He said he will," Keoghan responded. "Are you ready for our test?"

"Never. Let's do it."

Keoghan's Statistics final went surprisingly well, so much so that she knew she would keep a high grade in the class. She met with Celena and Iris outside of the hall to debrief as soon as they were dismissed.

"That was a mindfuck," Celena laughed loudly. "Jesus Christ."

Iris nodded. "I think I did alright, though."

"Yeah," Keoghan chimed in. "Same."

"No doubt I did well, I just hated it and it was confusing," Celena told them. "God, I need a hit."

"So there is doubt," Keoghan teased.

Celena flipped her off. "Bite me, Kay."

Iris smiled. "How about we go to the cafe for lunch as a celebration?"

"I have class all day on Tuesdays," Celena reminded her.

"Just us, then?" Iris asked, turning to Keoghan, who nodded. "Great. It's a date."

Once again, Keoghan felt her heart flutter. It was the first time she had felt it since Lukas's passing, and it felt strange. She felt like she didn't deserve to feel hope or love anymore. She had caused his death, and regardless of what others said she refused to give up that notion. Why should she be allowed to go on dates when her cousin would never know that they were dates? He would never know her identity. She could tell her head-demons, the hallucinations, whatever they were, to get some comfort, but they would never be Lukas. They could never love her like he did.

"Keoghan, you good?" Iris asked. "Sorry. Should I not have called it a date?"

Keoghan shook her head. "No, no. If you, uh, if you wanted it to be a date it could be."

Iris's eyes widened. "Oh. Shit. Yeah. It's a date, then. A real date."

"Eriyouneedtohelpmerightnow," Keoghan told her roommate, practically kicking down the door. "Eri. Eri. Eri!"

Eri pushed aside their noise-cancelling headphones and looked up. "What?"

"I'm going on a date with Iris."

"Seriously?" they cried. "Keoghan, that's amazing! She's liked you forever!"

Keoghan was taken aback. "Really?"

"Dude. Did you think she didn't?"

"Uh, yeah, kind of... But I corrected that stance today!"

Eri laughed. "I'm so happy for you. I wish Ben was the date type."

"He's just a fuckboy, Eri," Keoghan sighed. "You deserve better. So much better."

"He's nice to me, though."

"Eri... he's using you for a quick hookup. He doesn't actually care about you."

"How do you know that?" Eri asked defensively. "You've never interacted with him."

"Fine. You want to know how I know? He told Lukas that he would date him and then hooked up with you less than a day later," Keoghan told them.

Eri's eyes widened. "What the fuck? Keoghan, that's not funny."

"It's not a joke."

"Lukas- Lukas wasn't gay."

"Yes, he was," Keoghan responded. "Part of the reason he killed himself was living in secret for so long."

Eri leaned back in their chair and sighed. "I never would have known."

"That was the point."

"Jesus. Keoghan, why didn't you tell me sooner?"

"I figured you'd get over him."

Silence. Keoghan watched as Eri processed the information they had been given, and hoped that maybe, somehow, they would understand. She knew that Ben wasn't the single cause for Lukas's death, but she still blamed him. He had, in some way, taken her best friend from her. He didn't deserve happiness. He didn't deserve Eri.

"I'm so sorry, Keoghan," Eri finally whispered. "None of this is fair."

"I know," Keoghan responded.

"You can't blame Ben, though. He's a good person."

"Yeah, right," Keoghan snorted. "He doesn't deserve you."

Eri shook their head. "Let me have my fun. That's all Ben is to me: fun. Nothing's gonna happen."

"Just be careful."

"I know. I will."

18

Keoghan met Iris at the cafe after her second class, her palms sweaty and heart racing. It was a date. She was on a date.

"Hey," Iris greeted as Keoghan sat down. "How was class?"

"I have my final presentation on Thursday," Keoghan groaned.

"Good luck. I have one today."

Not knowing what to say, Keoghan simply nodded.

"Thank you for coming here with me," Iris said after a while. "And for, uh, making it a date."

Blush rose to Keoghan's cheeks. "Of course. I didn't know if you meant it as, like, a real date, so I had to ask."

"I've wanted to go on a date with you since we met," Iris admitted. "But then, in the car on the way to my parents', you said something about some girl and I lost my confidence."

"That girl was you," Keoghan told her.

Iris smiled and placed her hand on the table, tapping her fingers together. "I'm honored to be your bi awakening."

"I'm honored to be your, I don't know, first college crush," Keoghan laughed.

Reaching across the table, Iris took Keoghan's hand and held it tight. Keoghan smiled. She really liked Iris, and Iris liked her. Still, there was that voice in her head. She didn't deserve to be happy when Lukas could never feel happiness again. She didn't deserve to go on a date with someone when just a few months prior she had refused William.

"Hey," Iris said, noticing Keoghan's retreat inward. "Let's get food, okay? We can talk more after."

"Yeah. Let's."

After their food was served, Iris gave Keoghan a serious look. "How are you doing in terms of... eating? I know you didn't like the support group."

Keoghan nodded. "I'm... better. I'm trying to be better. The thoughts are receding a bit."

"Good," Iris smiled. "If there's ever anything I can do..."

"Thank you."

"Of course. You're... you mean a lot to me, and I'll do whatever I can to help you."

Keoghan was warm. Strange. She was almost never warm, not with her body running on empty. A strange light was beyond her closed eyes, and when they fluttered open she realized it was the sun.

She looked around, and found herself on a terrace of a large brick house in what appeared to be a vineyard. When she glanced at herself, she noticed that she was... curvy.

"What the fuck?" she whispered, attempting to circle her wrist with her finger and failing. No. No, no, no. What was going on? She was never unable to clasp her fingers together, not for as long as she could remember.

Taking a closer look, as close as she dared, Keoghan inspected her clothes. A wine-red dress and gold jewelry adorned her, and she felt that she was in wedge sandals beneath the dress. Her clothes hugged her body, accentuating every piece of fat that clung to her.

This couldn't be right. She would never let herself change this much.

As she reached up to touch her hair, she felt a tap on her shoulder.

"He's ready for you, Keoghan," an unfamiliar man smiled. "I'm not allowed to see him yet, so... tell him I've never been happier than I am right now."

Keoghan nodded slowly. "And where should I find... him?"

"Lukas's in the upper bedroom. Our bedroom."

The world stood still, and all the warmth drained from Keoghan's body. "Lukas?"

"Do you think he'd miss his own wedding?" a woman laughed, walking up next to the man. Keoghan recognized her instantly.

"Cassidy?"

"What'd ya think, hun? That I just disappeared? We were gettin' the bar ready an hour ago. Now, go on. Go see your cousin."

Keoghan gave a quick nod, tears threatening to assault her face as she sped into the house. It was all too much. Lukas was alive? He was getting married? He was in a bedroom that another man had called 'their' bedroom?

She ascended the stairs, not sparing a glance for her surroundings. It was clear to her that it was Lukas's house, shared with the man. Maybe with his friends. Maybe Keoghan lived a few minutes away. Maybe, maybe, maybe...

"Keo?" a voice called.

Keoghan steeled her nerves and bit her lip. She was going to see Lukas. He was alive. He was well. He was getting married.

"I'm coming," she replied, pushing open the door she thought she had heard him through. "I'm- Oh my God! Oh my fucking... Lukas!"

Lukas's voice echoed throughout the room.

"I'm sorry, I'm sorry, I'm sorry..."

He hung from the ceiling, wearing a suit of the same color as Keoghan's dress. He was ashen, his limbs limp, his eyes closed.

"Keo, I'm sorry..." his voice said. "I didn't want to leave you..."

"No," Keoghan sobbed, her knees giving out and causing her to collapse onto the hardwood floor. "I didn't want this. Lukas, no."

"I'm sorry, I'm sorry, I'm sorry..."

Keoghan woke with a start, her heart racing and hands clenched. She hugged her pillow to her chest and began to cry.

19

Finally, finally it was winter break. Keoghan packed her things and once again piled them into Iris's car, hoping that this visit to Portland would end on a better note than the last. Iris connected her phone to the car's Bluetooth system and handed it to Keoghan.

"Play whatever. I trust you."

Keoghan smiled. She was glad Iris liked and trusted her enough to have control of her phone. It was a refreshing feeling.

Scrolling through Iris's playlists, Keoghan saw many alternative songs that she wasn't familiar with. She exited playlist after playlist until she saw one that caught her eye.

K ◇

Her breath hitched, and she slowly clicked on the playlist. It was all the same music that had been in the rest of Iris's playlists, but this time she hit play. The first song that came on was *Climax* by Scene Queen, and Keoghan closed her eyes to listen.

"Nothing lasts forever, I've seen that. This feels like forever, so it makes me sad."

She felt a hand on hers, and opened her eyes. Iris was holding her hand, eyes on the road.

"I think you found your playlist."

Keoghan laughed. "I feel bad now, I didn't make one for you."

"Don't worry about it. I didn't expect you to."

"I'll love you until you die, you make me laugh 'till I cry. Can you swear on all your life that you'll be the exception, be the exception?"

Iris squeezed Keoghan's hand. "I hope you know that as long as you want me, I'll be around."

"I..." Keoghan's voice trailed off as she thought about her response. She wanted Iris around forever. She wanted to hold her, go to Portland with her, graduate with her. "I think I'll want you around forever."

"Then I'll stick around forever," Iris smiled.

"Don't let it end, don't let it end, don't let it end..."

Later in the drive, the two women decided to stop at a gas station to get food and drinks. Keoghan bought a protein bar and a Coke Zero, and Iris got a bag of edamame chips and a white Monster. They ate as they continued along the drive to Portland, music accompanying them in the background.

"You know, when I first came out as trans, my parents didn't like it," Iris told Keoghan. "They wanted me to be a successful businessman, and they thought that I couldn't do it as a woman. Not to mention that they had raised a son, not a daughter."

"But they came around? You said you went on puberty blockers, right?" Keoghan asked. "Sorry if that's rude."

"No, it's fine. I trust you enough to tell you things like this. They came around after I got a bit older, and really accepted it once I went on estrogen. I'm really lucky. I know a lot of families aren't as accepting as mine."

Keoghan laughed grimly. "Yeah. I know that, too."

"Firsthand experience with that for you, right?" Iris asked. "That's horrible."

"It was... it was one of the reasons why Lukas..."

Iris nodded solemnly. "Ah. He was... bi?"

"Gay. Fully gay, because he could commit to that. Unlike me," Keoghan sighed, shaking her head.

"It's not a commitment, or a choice," Iris told her. "You're committing to being who you are by saying you're bisexual. You don't have to be lesbian or trans to be part of the community. Bi people are giving just as much and have to experience just as many heartbreaks. Maybe even more."

Cracking a small smile, Keoghan leaned her head over and bumped it against Iris. "You always know exactly what to say."

"It's helpful having been there myself."

"Are you... bi, then?"

Iris shook her head. "I'm a lesbian, but I did think I was bi for a while. Part of me thought if I was a woman, I had to be attracted to men. It took me a long time to realize that trans girls could be lesbian, too."

"Cool. You're the second lesbian I've met, then." Keoghan laughed. "God, I need to get out more."

"We need to talk about this with the rest of our friends. I'm not going to come out for them, but almost all of them are queer as well, if not all of them."

"I know Eri's, uh... genderqueer? Is that the term?"

Iris smiled. "Yeah. Look at you, getting to know queer terminology."

"I'm learning," Keoghan laughed quietly. "Yeah."

They fell into silence for a while, soft music playing in the background. Keoghan ate her protein bar, Iris sipped her drink.

Eventually, Iris broke the silence.

"Keoghan?"

Keoghan looked over to her. "Yeah?"

"Why did you call Lukas 'Reg'?" she asked.

A faint smile appeared on Keoghan's face as the memories came flooding in. "God, that goes back to our childhood. He wanted to be a king and have me as his court jester, and we happened to be learning Latin at the time, so I started calling him Rex. Trouble was, I couldn't pronounce Xs correctly, so I called him Reg and it stuck."

"Too bad little Reg isn't going to be around for you, huh?"

Balling her fist, Keoghan clenched her jaw. William just wouldn't leave her alone.

"We're gonna get you. Don't think you're safe in Portland, almond milk bitch. You're going to pay."

Keoghan felt a hand on hers, and she closed her eyes. Iris was with her. William wasn't real. He couldn't hurt her. She was safe.

"William bothering you again?" Iris asked gently. Keoghan nodded. "Fuck off, William."

"Yeah," Keoghan agreed. "Fuck off."

The two woman sat in silence again, until Keoghan began to speak. "You know... I had a dream," she told Iris.

Iris nodded. "Good dream or bad dream?"

"Bad. Really bad," Keoghan sighed. "I was in this vineyard, and I was... fat. But that's not the problem. It was Lukas's wedding day, and his husband was there and told me to go see him. Cassidy was there. And... and..."

She began to shake, silent tears rolling down her cheeks.

"And when I went to see him, he hung himself."

Iris's eyes widened. "I'm so sorry, Keoghan. That's... that's fucked up. That's really fucked up."

"Yeah. I thought it would be a happy dream, and then I walked into his room and he..."

Keoghan felt a hand holding hers. She looked over and saw Iris's eyes filled with concern, though they were still fixed on the road.

Suddenly, a presence appeared behind her. The seat seemed to disappear, and she felt arms wrap around her, a head lean against hers.

"I'm always with you, Keo."

Keoghan reached up to touch the presence. It was warm, and it felt so real. So, so real.

"I'm always with you as well, Reg," she murmured. "Always."

Iris looked over to her. "Lukas?"

"Yeah. He's with me."

"We're all with you," Iris smiled. "But him especially. You're his legacy, Keoghan. You get to keep him with you until you see him again."

"Don't come for me soon, alright? I want you to live. Do all the things, drink all the drinks, and... Keo, please. Eat something."

Keoghan squeezed her eyes shut and nodded. "I'm going to try my best."

20

When they arrived, Iris's parents greeted them again.

"Baobao, Keoghan! Hello!" Meng Xin cried. "Your first semester of college, done!"

Iris smiled. "Yeah, Mama. I'm pulling a 4.0."

"As we'd expect from someone like you," her father smiled.

"Let's go eat dinner. Keoghan, how are you? How have you been feeling?" Meng Xin asked.

"I've been alright," Keoghan responded, following the family into the dining room. "Doing as best I can."

Meng Xin nodded. "Losing someone so precious is hard, but you are strong. There is nothing grief can't take from you. Don't let it take anything. Life will always find a way."

"Thank you, Meng Xin," Keoghan smiled. "That's really poetic. And good advice."

Returning the smile, Meng Xin pulled out a chair from the table. "I'm a mother. Of course I have good advice."

Keoghan woke up at 1 AM. Nothing she tried could get her back to sleep- taking the blanket off, switching to laying on her back, fluffing the pillow. She raked her hand through her hair and stared at the ceiling. If she were in her dorm, she would make tea. But she wasn't. She was in Iris's house, and whereas she knew that meant ultimate safety, she couldn't help but be worried about-

"Miss me, almond milk bitch?"

"Go away," Keoghan groaned. "Let me sleep."

"You know, refusing me after everything I've done for you? Really childish."

"Leave me the fuck alone."

"No," William crooned, leaning over Keoghan until his face nearly touched hers. *"I've given you so much. It's time you paid me back."*

"Iris! HELP!"

The door flung open, and Iris ran over to Keoghan's bed. "William, get the fuck out."

"Got a girlfriend, hmm? If I find out you let her do what I couldn't, even though I deserved it much more than that little tranny ever will, I'm coming for both of you."

Instead of shattering, William seemed to curl in on himself until he was no more, just a little ball of light that fizzled out.

"Are you okay?" Iris asked, taking Keoghan's hand. "Did William hurt you?"

Keoghan shook her head. "He never hurts me. He just tells me he will."

"Are you and Soledad working on it?"

"Yeah. We're doing EMDR for it," Keoghan told her.

Iris nodded. "Good. Let's go downstairs, I'll make you tea."

Keoghan eventually fell asleep on the couch, leaning on Iris.

After she woke up, Keoghan and Iris walked to a cafe for breakfast (as Iris's parents didn't eat in the mornings), chatting the whole way. As they sat down with their food, Iris sighed happily.

"I'm so glad you're here with me," she told Keoghan. "I love my parents, but sometimes holidays get lonely when it's just the three of us."

Keoghan nodded. "I get that. I'm really grateful that you let me come out here. I don't think I could survive being alone for the holidays, especially with Reg... gone."

"You're always welcome here. My parents text me and ask me when you're coming back all the time."

"Really?"

"Yeah," Iris laughed, pulling out her phone and opening a screenshot. "I meant to send this to you, I just forgot."

Mama: ⍰ ⍰⍰ ⍰⍰ ⍰ ⍰⍰⍰

"That means 'When is she coming back?'," Iris told her.

Keoghan smiled. Iris's family was becoming more and more like her own. "She really asks that?"

"All the time. She always forgets the dates that you're visiting, so I get that about once a week."

Iris reached across the table and took Keoghan's hand. Keoghan liked how she did it seemingly all the time; it made her feel valued. Loved. Like she mattered. And she knew that to Iris, she did matter. Now, she knew that she mattered to Iris's family as well.

"Iris?" Keoghan whispered, overcome with emotion.

"Yeah?"

"I know we're not even, well, I don't know what we are, but..." Keoghan murmured with a smile, "you make me feel like I matter. And I love that. And... I love you because you make me feel like you love me, too."

Iris stood up and knelt down next to Keoghan. "I love you, too. A lot."

Keoghan leaned down and touched her forehead against Iris's. "Can we... can we go on another date sometime?"

"Yes."

The emotions Keoghan had been afraid to feel since William's violation, since Lukas's passing, launched themselves at her like a grenade.

"Can I kiss you?"

"Yes," Iris breathed. "Please."

Keoghan took Iris's face in her hands and gently brushed their lips together. "I love you."

Iris kissed her back, placing her hands over Keoghan's. "I love you too."

21

Keoghan and Iris walked back to Iris's house hand in hand. The emotions from the cafe still crashed over Keoghan, tossing her about like waves on a beach. She had told Iris that she loved her. They had kissed. They were walking in public, holding hands.

She didn't know how to feel. Someone could see her touching another woman. They could see the look of complete adoration in her eyes. They could see where Iris's black lipstick had rubbed off on her, and (despite many washes in the cafe bathroom) hadn't come off. Despite knowing that nobody in Portland knew her or her family, or cared at all, she couldn't help but be afraid.

"Hey," Iris said softly, pausing to look at Keoghan and brush a strand of red hair out of her face. "You're tense. What's going on?"

Keoghan took a deep breath out. "I don't want people to think- well, to know- that I'm queer. My family will find out some way or another, and I can't let them."

Iris placed her free hand on Keoghan's cheek. "Nobody cares here. I promise. We're nothing unusual to them."

"I know that in theory, but... are you sure?"

"Yes. We're just as normal as anyone else."

"Okay," Keoghan breathed. "I trust you."

"You'd better," Iris laughed. "You're my... my Keoghan."

"I'll happily be your Keoghan anywhere, as long as I'm safe."

"You're always safe with me."

Later that day, the two women went to the Asian market with Meng Xin to buy the last ingredients for Christmas dinner. They were making *Huo Guo*, which Keoghan learned was hot pot, and so they wanted to get ingredients for everyone's personal requests.

"Let's see, Qiu wants pork, lotus, cabbage, noodles, and shrimp wontons. I'll take the same as him. Girls, what do you want?" Meng Xin asked, looking at a shopping list.

"Lotus, please," Iris responded immediately.

"We can share a pot," Keoghan suggested. "If Iris is ok with it, of course."

Iris nodded. "Let's get chicken, tofu, bok choy, lotus, and glass noodles?"

"Sounds great."

Keoghan tried not to think of the calories in the food. She had promised Lukas she would eat, and it was Christmas. She deserved to at least try the Huo Guo.

The women wandered through the aisles, looking for the things they wanted. Iris and Keoghan got lost in the frozen dumplings, looking at each box.

"I've never heard of some of these," Keoghan marveled. "They look so good..."

"Remind me to take you to my favorite Asian market near Stanford," Iris told her. "It's amazing."

"I'd love that. I've never really had a lot of Asian food, certainly not Chinese. My family was usually a white-people-food family."

Laughing, Iris took her hand as she always did, making Keoghan instantly feel at ease. "We'll have to go soon, then."

Meng Xin came bustling around a corner, carrying a shopping bag. "Alright, girls, let's go! We still have so much to do!"

Keoghan and Iris followed her to the register and then out of the market, talking about the Huo Guo and other Christmas festivities.

"I did some research," Keoghan began, "and I was wondering... does your family do anything for the Moon Festival?"

Iris smiled. "We make mooncakes and hang up lanterns. I'm sad I don't get to go home for it, but we have Thanksgiving for that."

"I hope you can go home one time, at least. Maybe if it coincides with a day one of your instructors takes off?"

"Yeah. That would be great. And, of course, I'd bring you with me."

A warm feeling blossomed in Keoghan's chest, and she held Iris's hand tighter. "I... thank you, Iris."

"Of course. I love you, and I want you as part of my family."

2 2

Christmas, time of joy. Time of love. Time of peace. Time of food. Time of "you've gained weight". Time of Keoghan's family being overly restricting as they prepared for their annual Christmas Gala.

"Remember, Keoghan, you are to dance with each son of the families we have invited at least once," her mother told her, just as she did every year. "And for God's sake, do something about that hair."

"Yes, mother."

"And wear the dress we picked out. Make sure you take advantage of the slits and neckline, we don't do these Galas for nothing. You will find a husband amongst these men."

Keoghan shuddered as she thought about the revealing dresses her mother chose, all designed to make her appealing to the sons of rich businessmen set to inherit the company. She always hated them, and she knew that now she would rather follow Lukas than wear one.

"That's a shame, I would have loved to see my little whore in a dress befitting for her. You just had to show yourself off to the men but never give them anything, didn't you? We all know that's what you do," William crooned, his icy fingers brushing her neck and jawline from behind. *"You're gonna pay, slut."*

Keoghan grabbed his wrist and pulled him in front of her. "Fuck you."

"You're getting bite, almond milk bitch. Too bad it's not enough. You know Iris will abandon you. You know everyone will die. If it's not your fault, it's because you're cursed. Oh, wait, that would mean that it was your fault. You're going to be the cause of everyone's death."

He laughed maniacally, and Keoghan kneed him in the crotch. The laughter stopped. The cold receded. William shattered, and Keoghan was alone on her bed.

Iris entered Keoghan's room. "Hey, Keoghan."

Keoghan looked up at her and smiled. "Hey, Iris."

"Merry Christmas! I hope you slept well."

"Same to you," Keoghan told her. "Downstairs?"

"Downstairs."

The two women descended the staircase and found themselves in the living room, where a brightly lit-up tree they had decorated a few days prior greeted them. Meng Xin and Qiu were in the kitchen. In all the Christmases Keoghan had experienced before, colorful trees or happy kitchen chatter were not part of them.

She followed Iris into the kitchen. As soon as they entered, Iris's parents descended.

"We don't do a lot of gift-giving in this house," Meng Xin explained to Keoghan, "but we decided to give you something."

Keoghan's eyes widened in shock. "Me? But I'm not..."

"You're family to us. Here, take it," Qiu told her, handing her a small box.

She opened it and gasped. The box contained a gold locket.

"I can't accept- this is-"

"Just open it," Iris murmured, placing a hand on Keoghan's shoulder. Keoghan did, and it felt like all the breath had been knocked out of her. Inside the locket was a picture of Lukas.

"Where did you get this picture?" Keoghan asked.

"I took it a few days before Thanksgiving break, remember?"

Keoghan, her friends, and Lukas stood in the Cantor art museum sculpture garden. They had just been inside the museum. Iris had her camera and was focused on Keoghan and Lukas as they smiled at a statue. Click.

Tears threatened to spill out of Keoghan's eyes, and she wrapped her arms around Iris. "Thank you so much."

She turned to Meng Xin and Qiu. "And thank you. This is..."

Meng Xin nodded. "Something to remember him by. He must have been very close to you."

"He was my best friend. My only family until I went to Stanford."

"Let me put it on for you," Iris suggested. Keoghan nodded, and lifted her hair off of her neck. Iris stepped behind her and clasped the necklace, her fingers brushing against Keoghan's skin. "There."

Reaching up to touch the locket, Keoghan leaned against her. "Thank you, all of you."

"Of course. Anything for our family, even if we are not bound by blood," Meng Xin smiled. "And trust me, that was a small thing."

Later that day, the family ate the leftover Huo Guo and chatted. Keoghan was, for the first time in her life, comfortable on Christmas. She felt no need to hide in her room, no need to hide her eating habits, no need to hide at all. She was home.

"Hey," Iris said quietly that night as she entered Keoghan's room, pulling her from her sleep. "I want to take you somewhere."

Keoghan rubbed her eyes and sat up. "It's one AM."

"Exactly," Iris smiled.

Laughing quietly, Keoghan got out of bed and followed Iris downstairs. They grabbed their coats and shoes and climbed into Iris's car.

A few miles later, the city lights had disappeared and the sky was dark. Keoghan could see something faintly glowing in the sky, something colorful.

"Is that...?"

Iris nodded. "The Aurora. It's really rare that it comes down here, but it did. Some people even saw it in Kansas."

"Wow," Keoghan breathed. "It's beautiful."

The lights reflected in Iris's eyes, and Keoghan took her hand. Iris pulled her close and kissed her.

"Merry Christmas, my Keoghan."

"Merry Christmas, Iris."

23

The departure from the Song house was hard. Keoghan was terrified to return to school after William tormented her every night and some days. It would get worse when she was near the place where everything happened, she just knew it. Still, she steeled her nerves and drove back to Stanford with Iris.

As soon as they hit the highway, Keoghan's phone began to explode with texts from Elizabeth and Chloe in their group chat.

Chloe: Keoghan

Chloe: Keoghan

Chloe: KEOGHANA KEOGHAN KEOFANG

[What]

Chloe: when are u gonna be here

Liv: How was your Christmas?

Chloe: keoghan you need to come back right now

Chloe: i miss u

[I'll be there soon]

[I have something to tell you]

Keoghan exhaled and closed her phone. She would do it. She would come out to her friends. Maybe she would tell them about Iris.

They weren't girlfriends. Not yet. But she was Iris's Keoghan, and that was more than enough.

When the women arrived on campus, they went to dinner with their friends in the dining hall.

"How was your Christmas, Kay?" Celena asked. "Do anything fun?"

Keoghan nodded. "I hung out with Iris."

"Fuck yeah. I got to beat my siblings' asses in soccer."

"As you should. I need to watch you play sometime."

"Yeah, you do."

Once everyone sat down, Keoghan took a deep breath and smiled. "Guys?"

Her friends' attention was captured.

"I have something... uh... I... I'm bisexual! I'm a queer."

Chloe, who sat across from her, laughed and smiled back. "Welcome to the gay group, then. We're all queer here."

"Really?" Keoghan asked. "Iris said that, but I didn't know."

Chloe nodded. "I'm lesbian and genderfluid. Liza is... pan?"

"Pansexual, trans woman," Elizabeth told Keoghan.

"Well, you know I'm genderqueer," Eri smiled.

"And I'm a lesbian... and asexual," Celena added.

Keoghan nodded. "I guess it was about time I realized, then. Thank you for telling me, all of you. And thank you for supporting me."

"Of course, Kay," Celena laughed. "You're part of the fucked-up family."

"I guess we are a fucked-up family," Eri mused. "We should have a family name."

"The Stanford Sapphics," Iris joked. "The Fags of Freedom."

"I like Fucked-Up Family," Chloe chimed in.

The group began to shout out ideas, vetoing or approving others'. Keoghan watched with a smile. Her friends were truly some of the best people she knew, and they had given her so much. She hoped that one day, hopefully not too distant, she would be able to return the favor.

Eventually, they decided on "The Gay Gals". Short, sweet, and PG.

The next day was New Year's Eve. Keoghan and her friends planned to go out to get sushi downtown as a celebration and a consolation that the new semester would start soon. As she was getting ready, Keoghan noticed that Eri wasn't.

"We have to leave in, like, half an hour," she told them. "Aren't you coming?"

Eri shook their head. "I'm... I'm not feeling like sushi."

"We can get you miso soup or something. Come on, you don't want to be alone on New Year's. It's a time for friends," Keoghan badgered. "Please?"

"I said I'd go to a party with Ben," Eri mumbled.

Keoghan groaned. "Jesus, Eri. Okay. I'm not mad. I'm not mad. But why?"

"Because he's cool! I promise."

"Cool as in going to ice you out once he gives you an STD or something."

"It's not- He's not going to give me an STD."

"Yes, he is," Keoghan sighed. "Are you even being safe?"

"You're not my mother, Keoghan," Eri spat. "And even if you were, I wouldn't care. Nothing bad is going to happen. Ben isn't like that."

Keoghan shook her head. "I'm just trying to make sure you don't get hurt."

"Yeah, well, try harder."

Eri stormed out of the room, and Keoghan assumed they were going to Ben's. She raked a hand through her hair and leaned against the wall. Something bad was going to happen. She could feel it.

"Oh, don't worry," William cackled. *"He's a good person. Just like me."*

Chills ran down Keoghan's spine. Eri was going to get hurt. She had to do something, anything, whatever she could.

Just as she was about to find someone to interrogate for Ben's dorm number, her phone chimed. It was the group chat.

Liv: Soshi

Liv: sent a GIF (alt text: a cat is picked up by the scruff of its neck and has a piece of sushi in its mouth with the caption 'soshi'.)

Eri: not gonna make it tonight sorry

Liv: It's fine. Are you sick?

Eri: no i forgot i had other plans

Eri: keoghan should be coming tho

Keoghan sighed and typed a response.

[Yeah, I'm coming]

By the time the group arrived at the restaurant, sat down, and ordered, Keoghan was on edge. Eri could be getting seriously hurt. And if William had shown his face... she wondered if that was the stress, or if it was a sign of something. Eri trusted Ben. Keoghan did not.

"Do you know where Eri is?" Elizabeth asked. "They said they had other plans?"

Keoghan grimaced. "Ben."

"Still? I thought that shit was dead," Celena commented, stirring her green tea with her fork. "Jesus, I'm hungry."

"Didn't we all?" Chloe sighed.

"Let's just eat our sushi and leave it alone. Eri's an adult. It'll be fine," Celena told the group.

Everyone nodded, though an air of discomfort surrounded them. Keoghan felt sick, her stomach churning and head spinning. Eri *was* an adult, and maybe they should leave it alone, but they could get hurt. Seriously hurt.

Their rolls arrived, and the group ate in silence. Keoghan wasn't the praying type, she wasn't even religious, but she desperately wanted someone who was out there who would listen to her concerns. Someone who would tell her that Eri would be fine, Ben wouldn't hurt them, anything. Any reassurance.

"Eri's probably getting murdered right now," William sang into Keoghan's ear. *"They're getting the shit beaten out of them and fucked while they're down. You know they are."*

Keoghan clenched her hands around her chopsticks. She wouldn't dignify William with a response.

"Keo, it's okay. Eri's okay."

She whipped around. Lukas was standing behind her, smiling.

"I promise. Everything will work out like it has to."

"Thanks, Reg," she whispered. "Thank you."

"Kay. You good?" Celena asked, reaching across the table to poke Keoghan's shoulder.

Keoghan nodded. "Yeah. I'm good. Where do we want to go after we eat?"

"Fireworks!" Chloe smiled. "I want to see fireworks."

2 4

After they finished their sushi, the group walked to a park on campus to watch fireworks. As soon as they sat down, Keoghan's phone rang. She looked at who was calling her; it was Eri.

"Hey," she greeted. "What's going on?"

Eri's voice came out in sobs. "Keoghan... I... can you pick me up? I'm in front of the housing complex at the edge of campus."

Keoghan nodded. "Of course. Do you want me to bring everyone else?"

"No. Just you."

"Alright. I'm on my way."

"Keoghan?"

"Yeah?"

"Can you..." Eri sniffed, "can you stay on the phone with me?"

"Of course," Keoghan smiled. "I'm coming to get you."

When she arrived at the housing complex, Keoghan saw a disheveled and shaking Eri standing in the light of the streetlamp.

"What happened?" she asked, running over to them. "Did Ben hurt you?"

"Keoghan... Keoghan, I'm pregnant."

Keoghan's eyes widened, and she wrapped Eri in a hug. "Because of Ben?"

"Yes. I'm so sorry. I should have listened to you and cut things off..." Eri sobbed. "I'm so sorry."

"It's okay. You didn't know. Everything's going to be alright."

Footsteps sounded behind them, and Keoghan turned around. A short man with slicked back brown hair approached them, carrying a leather jacket.

"You forgot this," he told Eri. "You left so quickly."

Keoghan took the jacket and stared him down. "Who are you?"

"Call me Balthy, dear female."

"Balthy?" Keoghan laughed. "Alright. Well, Balthy, thank you. Now leave. I'm taking Eri home."

"I'm sure she can get home alright. Why don't you stay?"

"No. I'm taking *them* home. Goodnight."

Keoghan took Eri's hand and led them away.

"Bitch!" Balthy called as they left.

"Ignore him," Eri mumbled. "He's a dick."

Keoghan nodded. "Noted. What happened tonight?"

"I started feeling really sick, and everything was hurting, and then I remembered that... that a few weeks ago, we hadn't used protection. So I went to the store and took a test, and..." Eri began to shake even more. "I'm so sorry."

Keoghan stopped and placed her hand on their shoulder. "It's okay. It's not... well, it is your fault, but it's also Ben's. Have you talked about it with him?"

"He said it wasn't his and broke things off."

"What a dick. Alright, okay. What do you want to do now?"

Eri balled their fist. "I'm going to get an abortion."

"Okay. There's a Planned Parenthood in Redwood City. I'll drive you as soon as we can," Keoghan told them.

"You don't have a car."

"Iris does. I won't tell her what we're doing if you don't want to, but I'll borrow hers."

"Alright. Thank you, Keoghan," Eri sighed.

"Of course. Come on, let's get home."

Keoghan drove Eri to Planned Parenthood a few days later. She waited as they were called in, and when they came back out they were shaking.

"I can't believe I did it," they whispered to Keoghan as they exited. "I took a pill, and I have to take another one tomorrow, and then it's over."

Keoghan pulled them into a hug and held them tightly. "You're taking back your power. I'm so proud of you."

"Thank you. I'm... I don't know. Part of me wonders what would have happened if I kept the pregnancy."

"If you want to talk it out on the drive, you can. Just don't guilt yourself over it. You made the right decision."

Eri nodded and buried their head in Keoghan's shoulder. "Thank you. I think... I think we should go home."

"Yeah. Let's go."

They walked to Iris's car, and Keoghan opened the passenger door for Eri. She climbed in on the driver's side and turned on the car.

"What would you have done if I kept it?" Eri asked quietly. "Would you still have been my friend?"

"Of course," Keoghan told them. "There is nothing in this world that will keep me from being your friend, and accidental pregnancy is far from the worst. I might disapprove of your choices, but I won't let them come between us."

Eri nodded. "Thank you."

"There isn't anything to thank me for. I'm just being a good friend."

The next day, Keoghan woke up to find Eri gone. She texted them, asking where they were. No response. Climbing down from her bed, she saw a note on her desk.

Keoghan,

I'm safe. I'm just going for a walk.

Keoghan ran a hand through her hair and crumpled the note in her hand. After Lukas, she wasn't sure if she could handle any of her friends disappearing without a note, so she was glad that Eri had taken the time, especially after the ordeal they had just been through.

"Oh, I do love the taste of a fresh soul," she heard an unfortunately familiar voice croon behind her.

"What do you mean?" she asked slowly.

"You'll see. Why don't we take a walk, just like dear Eri?"

Dread pooled in her stomach, and she ran out of the room. In the common area, the students were gathered in a circle. She walked over to them.

"What happened?" she asked.

One of the students turned to her, face ashen. "They found someone dead in the road. A hit-and-run. The police is outside."

"Who was it?"

"Someone named Eri Hernandez. A Physics major."

All the blood ran out of Keoghan's face. No. *No.*

"That... are you sure?" she whispered. The student nodded.

Fuck.

ACT THREE:
BLOOM

25

ERI'S INTERLUDE

Keoghan attended Eri's funeral and sat in the back. Nobody noticed her. Nobody spoke to her. She stood over their grave for a long time, holding a yellow rose in her hand. It hadn't had the thorns taken off, and they pierced her skin, but she didn't care.

If only she had woken up earlier. If only she had said something to help Eri. If only she had heard them, stopped them from going on a walk. If only...

"Hey," she heard Iris say next to her. "You ready?"

Keoghan took one last glance at the coffin in the ground and let the rose fall. It hit the wood with a thud.

"Goodbye, Eri," she murmured, scanning the other roses resting on the coffin.

A warm presence appeared next to her. *"Thank you for looking out for Keo."*

She felt Lukas's presence squeeze her hand, and she took a deep breath in, turning to Iris.

"Yeah. Let's go."

She followed Iris to where the rest of their friends waited around Iris's car. Chloe gave her a comforting smile, Elizabeth hugged her, and Celena sat in the back of the car with her.

"It's unfair," Celena told her as they made their way out of the cemetery. "You didn't deserve to have them taken. Their family didn't."

"But it happened anyway," Keoghan laughed grimly, staring out the window.

"It'll get better."

"I know."

Celena fell silent, and Keoghan continued watching the cemetery breeze past her. Someday, she would end up in a grave of her own.

Part of her hoped that day would be soon.

She wondered how it would happen. She didn't want to have her life taken from her forcibly, but suicide didn't seem right. Maybe she would die from her eating disorder.

The thought felt comforting. She was in control, but she wasn't completely at fault.

Keoghan decided that if she were to die young, she wanted to die at the hands of anorexia.

26

After Eri's funeral, Keoghan felt empty. She was waiting, watching her remaining friends, wondering who would be taken from her next. Maybe it would be Chloe. Lord knew how much longer she had left, how much life was still in her broken body. Maybe Celena. Her vaping problem could give her cancer, though Keoghan was unsure on how exactly that would work. Maybe even Elizabeth.

Maybe it would be Iris.

Keoghan hoped with every ounce of her being that it wouldn't be Iris.

Keoghan, Iris, and Celena waited for their instructor to come in their Financial Accounting class, Keoghan leaning on Iris and holding her hand.

"My room feels so lonely now that Eri's stuff got moved out," she mumbled. "I miss having a roommate."

Iris held her hand tighter and brought it up to her face. "I'm sorry, Keoghan. Next year, we'll rent an apartment, and you'll have a roommate again."

"Have you talked to Soledad about this?" Celena asked. Keoghan nodded.

"Eri was killed," she told Soledad. "I feel like I'm cursed, and William keeps telling me that I am. Everyone around me is dying. I can't..."

"Are you experiencing any suicidal thoughts right now?" Soledad asked.

Keoghan thought about it. She didn't want to kill herself, but she wanted to die. She had wanted to die for a long time.

"No."

Sighing, Keoghan buried her face in the crook of Iris's neck. Iris held her close, and she was comforted by the feeling of her shoulders rising and falling with her breath.

"We haven't gone on a date in a while," Keoghan murmured. "Do you want to go to a cafe soon? Something for distraction."

Iris nodded. "I would love that. Today over lunch?"

"Sounds good."

"It's a date, then," Iris smiled.

The two women met at the same cafe they always did, Keoghan arriving first for a change. As she waited for Iris, she saw a man approach out of the corner of her eye. It was Balthy.

"Hello, dear female," he said nasally. "Are you here alone?"

"I'm waiting for my girlfriend," Keoghan told him. Iris wasn't *technically* her girlfriend, but maybe it would scare Balthy away.

"I didn't know you were a lesbian. That's hot. Maybe I'll be a woman, then."

"She's taken, asshat," Iris said, walking over. "And we're not here for your fetishization."

Balthy glared at her and stalked away. "Fuckass dykes."

"Are you okay?" Iris asked Keoghan. "Who was that?"

"He knew Eri. For some reason, he wants to be with me."

Iris shook her head. "Fuck that kid."

"Seriously," Keoghan sighed.

"Not to change the topic, but I brought you something," Iris smiled.

"Oh?" Keoghan asked. Iris nodded, handing her a blood-red rose.

"It matches your bangs."

Keoghan smiled. Iris always knew how to make her feel better. "Thank you. I love it."

"I got you this because I, uh... I wanted to ask you, and I feel like now is the time, especially with that dick... would you want to be my girlfriend?" Iris asked.

"I would love to," Keoghan cried, walking over to Iris to hug her. "Thank you for loving me enough to ask."

Iris nodded. "Of course. Thank *you* for loving me enough to say yes."

She kissed her tenderly, and Keoghan reveled in the feeling of being loved. It was good. Pure. Soft, warm... she didn't know attraction could feel like this.

"I love you," she murmured. "So much."

"I love you, too."

Keoghan got a call from Elizabeth one night as she was walking back to the dorms.

"Hey, Keoghan," Elizabeth greeted. "Sorry for calling you out of the blue."

"It's alright," Keoghan smiled.

"I wanted to make sure you were safe. Eri... can't tell us when you get back safe anymore, so I decided to call you. I know walking around at night can be hard."

Keoghan nodded. "Thank you, Liv. I appreciate it. I'm fine right now, but I am worried about-"

"Hey! You!"

"*Fuck*," Keoghan whispered. "Balthy."

A shadow crossed Elizabeth's face. "Turn your volume up and take out your earbuds."

Keoghan did as she said, and Elizabeth cleared her throat.

"Hey, kid!" she called in a deep voice, one that Keoghan imagined was her natural voice before she trained it. "Leave her the fuck alone. This is her boyfriend, and I'm giving you one more chance to back the fuck up."

Balthy narrowed his eyes. "Oh yeah?"

"Keoghan, do you still have the knife I gave you?"

Elizabeth had never given Keoghan a knife, but Keoghan nodded anyway. "Of course, baby."

"A knife? You- you're insane!" Balthy cried, backing away. "I'll get you soon, bitch. Tell your boyfriend Balthy's coming for him."

He strode away, casting glances over his shoulder, and Keoghan plugged her earbuds back in.

"Thanks, Liv," she smiled. "I can't get that dick off my back."

"It's no problem. I'll be your fake boyfriend anytime."

Celena, Iris, and Keoghan sat in Iris's floor commons, Iris's laptop plugged into the TV to watch *Stranger Things*, which Keoghan hadn't seen. They had finished the first and second seasons over the past few meetups, and they were on to Season Three.

"Steve, man," Keoghan sighed, drinking a canned sparkling water. "He's so..."

"Is disgusting the word you're looking for? Robin's right there!" Celena cried.

Iris pursed her lips and nodded. "No, I get it. Steve's, like, man pretty."

Celena crumpled her empty can and tossed it aside. "You guys have horrible taste."

"No, you're just too man-phobic," Keoghan laughed.

"Damn right I am. Men are the worst thing to be created next to, I don't know, goats."

"What's wrong with goats?" Iris asked in mock offense. "You know, my great-grandma was a goat!"

"Try working on a farm and having to explain goats in heat to five-year-olds!" Celena sighed, shaking her head. "Never again."

Keoghan's eyes were glued to the screen.

"She is awesome. And what about the guy?"

"I think he's on drugs and not thinking straight."

"Really? Because I think he's thinking a lot more clearly than usual."

"Did Steve just fucking confess to Robin?" Keoghan cried. "No, Steve, no... I'm right here, Steve..."

"Hey, what about me?" Iris gasped with a grin. "And just wait."

"It isn't because I had a crush on you. It's because she wouldn't stop staring at you."

"Mrs. Click?"

"Tammy Thompson. I wanted her to look at me, but she couldn't pull her eyes away from you and your... stupid hair."

"Wait, guys..." Keoghan gasped, pointing at the screen. "Is Robin gay?"

"Tammy Thompson? But she's a girl."

"Steve..."

Keoghan turned to Iris. "Oh my fucking God." She turned to Celena. "Holy shit. Robin's gay."

"She truly is one of us," Celena sang.

"God, imagine being queer in the 80s... you could never have something like what we do, at least not publicly," Keghan sighed.

Iris reached over to take her hand. "It's important we have things like this. Imagine what a life, what joy Lukas could have had if he was with us now. The things you could have done if you had us when you were growing up."

"I know. I... I can't take anything for granted anymore," Keoghan nodded. "We can all be each others' Steves and Robins."

Celena smiled. "I'll be Robin's girlfriend, you mean."

"Yeah. You'll be Robin's girlfriend."

<h1 style="text-align:center">27</h1>

Keoghan couldn't escape Balthy's presence, even with Elizabeth as her "boyfriend". She walked to class, he was on the way. She went to the dining hall, he stood in front waiting for someone. It was suffocating.

"He's a nice guy," William told her.

"Shut. The fuck. Up," Keoghan groaned.

William chuckled and traced her jawline with his icy finger. *"Too bad I couldn't be the one in his place."*

Grabbing his arm, Keoghan threw him against the ground and he shattered, his manic laugh ringing in her ears even after he was gone.

One day, as she was walking to her Physics class, Balthy shouted her name from across the walkway.

"How did you learn my name?" she called back.

"From a friend."

"Okay, well, leave me the fuck alone."

"No," he laughed, stepping closer. "I don't think I will. You know, I heard from a few guys I know that one William Lucie killed himself because of a Freshman. Now, I didn't know anything about this Freshman except that she was a snake. She would flirt with you, lead you on, and then back out. Later, I hear them say that her family member committed as well. Serves her right, she gets to know how it feels. Now, guess whose roommate dies after disappearing with her? Pathetic. You're going to pay for all the lives you've taken, and all the people you treated the same way you did William. Myself included."

Backing away, Keoghan shook her head. "I didn't lead you on. I never interacted with you."

"You did with your eyes. You're a nasty bitch, Keoghan Winchester."

Balthy grabbed her arm and pulled her so close that she could feel (and smell) his breath on her face. She clawed at him, hit him with her free hand, kicked him, but he did not let go. Remembering the self-defense keychain she had bought after William, Keoghan reached into her pocket, looped her fingers through the holes of the cat design that hung off of her key strap, and brought the pointed ends up to Balthy's eyes. He doubled over in pain, letting her go, and she ran as fast as she could. No amount of distance seemed far enough. He could always come back. He could find her. She needed to leave.

"Run, run, little slut," William jeered. *"You won't escape your fate. You're a plaything for us, and that's all you'll ever be. If he doesn't get you, I will. Lukas will. Eri will. We're going to come for you."*

Keoghan pressed the keychain into her own palms. She needed the pain. Pain would make William go away. Pain would make her have the strength to keep running. Pain. She ran faster, her legs screaming and feet thundering against the ground. Pressing the keychain harder, she felt her heartbeat race as the world around her blurred. Nothing felt real.

When she finally stopped running, Keoghan noticed that she had broken the skin on her palm. She didn't care. She needed to get away. Somewhere. Anywhere.

Her phone vibrated.

Chloe: keoghan where tf are you

Chloe: are you ok

Celena: hey steve simp you need to get here right now

Iris: Keoghan? Where are you?

Taking a deep breath, Keoghan's heartbeat began to slow. Right. She had to go to class. But she couldn't go back. Not with Balthy on campus, looking to hurt her, not with William in her head. She knew she couldn't just disappear, not now that she'd made such strides with her friends and with Iris, but she had to leave. Balthy would find her. William would kill her. She wasn't safe on campus anymore.

[I'm going to go away for a bit. I'll be back soon.]

ACT FOUR: DECAY

28

Memories

"Keoghan Winchester?"

ˈ Whatever pounds of fourteen-year-old Keoghan remained sat in a weighted beanbag, staring at the wall with a blank expression on her face. The wall was bare.

"Are you Keoghan?"

She nodded and wondered if the rest of the unit was decorated as sparsely as the entryway.

"Alright. Welcome to Seasons of Growth! I'm Maddie, and I'll be your nurse today."

Keoghan said nothing.

"I'm sure they told you, but dinner will be at six today. After that, you'll have free time- visitation is on Mondays, Wednesdays, Fridays, and Sundays- and your night snack. Bedtime is at ten."

"And if I don't eat?" Keoghan asked, her eyes still not moving from the gray wall.

"You'll be given a meal replacement shake, and if you don't drink it you'll get the tube with 150% of the replacement shake in it. We don't operate calorie-to-calorie like the hospital does, we go by percentages. 0, 25, 50, 75, and 100. If you eat 24 percent of your meal, you'll be given the shake as if you'd had none."

Glaring at Maddie, Keoghan lifted herself from the chair, vision cutting out. After she steadied herself, she folded her arms. "That's fucking stupid. I want to go back to the hospital."

"No-can-do. I promise, it'll be fine here. You just have to try," Maddie smiled encouragingly.

Keoghan rolled her eyes. "Where's my stuff?"

"It's in your room. I'll show it to you."

Maddie led her into the main unit, painted a similar gray color but with more decoration and furniture. A group of girls sat around a table. Keoghan counted two tubes, five pairs of protruding collarbones, five gaunt faces. She balled her fist. They'd call her fat. They'd ridicule her. She'd never be allowed to socialize with them.

One girl gave her a small wave.

Looking away, Keoghan continued to follow Maddie to a fork in the road. A large area in between the halls was taken up by a half-wall where several people Keoghan assumed to be nurses sat and stood.

"One side leads to the dining room, conference rooms, and med room. The nursing station is this ugly thing. Just so you know, we have cameras everywhere except the bathrooms, so don't think you can sneak anything by us just because we're not in your rooms," Maddie explained.

Keoghan nodded. "Got it. Can we keep going?"

Maddie set herself back into motion and led Keoghan down the right hallway. One set of doors was placed on opposite sides of the hallway about 15 feet apart from the next, and there were four doors in total. Each door had a whiteboard with space for two names on it.

Mimi (1A), Loura (1B).

Jay (2A), Alice (2B).

Nick (3A), Keoghan (3B).

Keoghan reached for the door handle to the room and looked at Maddie. "Is this my room?"

"It certainly has your name on it," Maddie chirped. "You're the B side of the room, so the far side. Your things should be on your bed."

Light footsteps sounded in the hallway, and Keoghan turned around. A short girl with blonde hair in braids and deep blue eyes smiled up at her.

"My roommate's finally here! They said I'd get one today. I'm Nick, as you might have guessed."

Keoghan nodded slowly. "Hi."

"Do you want to unpack, or do you want to see the others?" Nick asked.

"I guess I'll see the others?"

Nick turned to Maddie and seemed to give her puppy-dog eyes. "Can she please come sit with us?"

Maddie nodded. "Of course. Let me just explain the rules first." She turned to Keoghan. "No explicit conversation about your eating disorder or self-harm, that means numbers or behaviors. No inappropriate topics. Try to steer clear of details regarding your treatment to avoid competition."

"Is that it?" Keoghan sighed. "Can we try something like, I don't know, not drowning us in rules?"

"Nope. You're here for a reason. Oh, and no touching."

Nick extended her hand and pretended to pat Keoghan's shoulder, keeping her palm an inch away from the other girl's shoulder. "You'll get used to it. Come on, let's go."

Keoghan followed her back down the hallway to the common area where the other four girls sat. A puzzle was laid out on the coffee table, and some of them appeared to be working on it. Keoghan gingerly sat down on a pillow on the ground, hugging her knees into her chest.

"Your hair is really pretty," one of the girls mumbled. "Mine is falling out. I wish it looked like yours."

Reaching a hand up to touch her shoulder-length hair, Keoghan shrugged. "I guess. I think it's kind of ruined because of the bleach and developer."

She had dyed the ends of her hair emerald green a few weeks prior, and whereas it wasn't too faded it certainly wasn't what it had been.

"It looks good to me. Very, uh, reverse Billie Eilish."

Keoghan nodded. "That wasn't the goal, but I'm happy to be compared to her."

"I'm Mimi," the girl told her. "You're Keoghan, right?"

"Yeah."

"Well, welcome. The others will warm up to you; they're shy at first. I'm happy to have you here," Mimi smiled.

"Thanks," Keoghan responded. She wasn't sure what to make of Mimi or of the clinic. At least she wouldn't be there for long.

Six months and several escape attempts later, Keoghan's bags were packed and she left Seasons of Growth. Nobody said goodbye; all the people she was with at the start had either been discharged or sent somewhere else. There was no clinical reason for her to leave, but the insurance company sure felt it was time for one to exist. So, Keoghan crossed her legs in the backseat of an Uber taking her home.

She had learned nothing.

29

KEOGHAN'S INTERLUDE

"On lead-poisoned wings, you try to sing..."

"Come on, babe," eighteen-year-old Keoghan heard a man groan beside her, drowning out her mind's song, "let's get outta here before the pigs show up. Do your thing."

She nodded, using her phone's flashlight to locate a vein on her arm. "The stuff, Finch?"

Finch chuckled and handed her a syringe and needle. "Always so impatient. I like it. It's sexy."

"You're a manwhore, you know," Keoghan laughed, angling the needle at 20 degrees and inserting it. When she removed it, she smiled at the blood beading on her skin. Pain. Pain was good. Pain made everything go away.

The feeling of the drug entering her bloodstream relieved the pain, but it also prevented the thoughts from coming back.

"The peacock screaming eyes, show no mercy, no mercy..."

She looked around the alley they were in. It was dark, with crumbling bricks of shops that didn't care about this side of their facade surrounding them. A stack of old newspapers lay on the ground, soggy. Keoghan always enjoyed reading the headlines- **PRESIDENTIAL ADMINISTRATION UNDER ATTACK? EVERYTHING TO KNOW ABOUT THE NEWEST TRIAL.**

"Alright, Sunnie, let's go," Finch said. Keoghan nodded, and he extended his hand to help her up. She loved that feeling- touching his rough hands, being called Sunnie, the feeling of feeling nothing.

"Just a tainted bird, hurting their twisted nerve..."

"Sonata. Come on."

"You never call me that," Keoghan sighed as they walked away.

Finch shrugged. "It is your real name."

"*Middle* name."

"Yeah, 'cause you won't tell me your first."

"Isn't Sonata enough for you?" Keoghan asked. "You already have every other part of me. A woman needs to keep something secret."

"As if your past wasn't enough," Finch chuckled. "Nah, it's fine. We all have to have our secrets."

Keoghan nodded. She refused to talk about any part of her life before she ran away from Stanford two and a half months prior. The only thing Finch knew was that he found her on the streets of Palo Alto at night, and that he took her in to live with him and his ex-girlfriend. They had taken her with them when they shot up, and eventually her thoughts became too loud, so she joined in. He didn't know that she sent her friends pictures of Europe that she found deep on the internet to keep them off her trail. He didn't know that she sometimes wanted to go back, but couldn't get herself to.

"Painted bird, it's absurd..."

As they walked down the street to their house, Keoghan spotted a flash of red hair in her peripheral vision. The flash turned around with wide eyes.

"Kay? Is that you?"

Fuck. The music in Keoghan's mind came to an abrupt stop.

"Finch, go ahead. I'll be right behind you," she told Finch, who nodded. As soon as he was out of earshot, Celena wrapped her arms around Keoghan and held her tight.

"I missed you. What are you doing back here without telling us?"

"I, uh..."

"And you've lost so much weight. You're bony to the touch, even more than normal. You look like a corpse. And your hair is in a bun. And your roots are grown out. And... and you look high. Kay..." Celena's voice quavered, and she took a step back. "Kay, did you really go to Europe?"

Keoghan said nothing, tears threatening to fall from her eyes.

"Kay. Alright. We're getting you back to campus. Now."

"No, I- Finch will worry-"

"No. You're coming with me. I have a car now, it's just around the corner," Celena told her firmly, grabbing her hand. "We're going to get this figured out."

"But- I can't go back to campus. Balthy will be there," Keoghan whispered.

"You mean Balthy, the Senior? He got kicked out for sexual assault charges," Celena said gently. "I'd imagine that would make sense to you?"

Keoghan nodded, feeling a massive weight off of her shoulders. "Yes. Yes, it would."

Celena smiled softly. "You're going to be alright. We have two months left of school, and then you can live off-campus with Iris... and me."

"Okay."

They arrived at the car, and Celena watched from outside as Keoghan got in. Keoghan felt like a psych patient, knowing her friends would treat her like glass. Especially if they knew that-

"Kay, you're tugging your sleeves down so much that your shoulders are showing."

Fuck.

"You... you have marks on your shoulder," Celena noticed slowly. "And... is that why you're tugging down your sleeves, too?"

Again, Keoghan said nothing.

"Kay..."

"I'm sorry, Celena," Keoghan whispered. "I'm so sorry."

Celena took her hand and held it tight. "It's okay. You're still with us. You're going to get better. I'm going to take you to Iris's dorm now, and we'll call Chloe and Elizabeth. We're going to make sure this doesn't happen again."

Keoghan nodded in silence.

"Here," Celena told her, handing Keoghan her phone. "Play music. Anything to get you home."

There was only one song Keoghan had listened to recently that she enjoyed.

"And even though the moment passed me by, I still can't turn away because all the dreams you never thought you'd lose got tossed along the way..."

It played in her head even after she arrived back on campus.

"You could hide beside me, maybe for a while, and I won't tell no one your name..."

It played in her head as her friends discussed what to do with her.

"Scars are souvenirs you never lose, the past is never far. Did you lose yourself somewhere out there? Did you get to be a star?"

It played in her head as she packed her bags with all the things that had been left to gather dust in her dorm room.

"You grew up way too fast and now there's nothing to believe, and reruns all become our history. A tired song keeps playing on a tired radio, and I won't tell no one your name..."

It played in her head as Iris drove her to an inpatient clinic near campus after re-enrolling her for the next fall semester.

"It's lonely where you are, come back down, and I won't tell 'em your name."

The song ended as she kissed Iris goodbye, tears streaming down both of their cheeks and intermingling in the space between them.

"I'll pick you up soon," Iris whispered. "We'll start again."

Keoghan nodded. "I love you, Iris."

"I love you too, my Keoghan."

Footsteps sounded behind them, and a smiling woman approached. "Keoghan Winchester?"

"Yeah?"

"It's time. I'll help you with your bags."

"Alright," Keoghan responded, steeling her nerves and giving Iris one last hug. "I'll see you soon."

"Yeah. Until then, my Keoghan."

"Until then, Iris."

ACT FIVE:
OVERWINTER

30

Keoghan entered the residential portion of the clinic at 3:34 PM. She knew that because of the giant clock that hung in the hallway. The woman led her through a maze of hallways, each outfitted with a similar clock, until they went through two large doors and the floor plan opened. The doors closed behind them, and they stood in a living-room-type space where four other women sat.

"Everyone," the woman called, "meet your new companion. This is Keoghan."

"Hi, Keoghan," the group chorused.

"Come sit down," a black-haired woman dressed in entirely pink said. "We don't bite."

"Anymore," another, a woman with short green hair laughed.

Keoghan walked over to them and sat down on an overly plush chair.

"Well, I'll bring your bags to your room. It's the second one down this hall, you'll be sharing with Siobhan."

"I'm Siobhan," the green-haired woman greeted. "Howdy."

"Hey," Keoghan mumbled.

"So," the pink-clad woman smiled. "I'm Reb. The other two are Alyssa and Mickie."

Keoghan nodded to the other women, who gave her no response.

"Sorry about them. They came in together after, uh, witnessing one of their friends OD. They don't talk much."

"It's alright," Keoghan said slowly. "I... I hope they get better?"

"Don't we all..."

"Ladies, the kitchen is open for a snack if anyone wants one," a booming voice called. "Dinner is in two hours, and we will be taking weights tomorrow, so make sure you're eating enough!"

Reb sighed. "They monitor our weights here. So many of us either have eating disorders or lost a lot of weight, so we're all on a weight gain diet."

"Great," Keoghan sighed. Weight gain? That was the last thing she wanted, the main reason she didn't want to go inpatient.

"You'll get used to it," Siobhan told her. "And once you're at a healthy weight-slash-not losing too much, your meal plan gets reduced. You can also ask the dietician for modifications. Do you have your own therapist?"

"I used to...?"

"You'll be seeing them through telehealth. Those of us who don't get one assigned from here."

Keoghan nodded. There was so much information coming at her.

"Well, I'm going to go see if they still have fruit cups," Siobhan smiled. "Anyone coming with?"

Steeling her nerves, Keoghan nodded. "I will."

That night, Keoghan and Siobhan took turns getting ready in the bathroom attached to their room. Siobhan was softly singing as Keoghan changed.

"Achilles, Achilles, Achilles, come down, won't you get up off, get up off that roof?"

Keoghan only had short-sleeved nightshirts, and she walked out of the bathroom with her arms tucked close to her body.

"You don't need to hide it," Siobhan told her gently, stopping her song. "I've been there, too. We all have."

Keoghan slowly unfolded her arms. It was the first time she had truly looked at them when she wasn't shooting up or adding more cuts, and she took in the sheer amount of marks she had created, knowing there were more that were hidden.

"I don't know how to stop," she whispered, turning them over to inspect the other side. "Even now, when I know I can't, it feels wrong. I can't go to bed without doing it."

Siobhan nodded. "I get that. It gets better, in time. The thoughts and the urges never go away, but it gets better. That's what we're all here for. To get better."

Keoghan flopped on her bed and stared at the room's ceiling. "Does it work?"

"Not if you don't want it to."

"I want it to."

"Do you, really? You have to *want* it. No more drugs, not ever. No more cutting, no more drinking, no more smoking, not even hitting a pen. Certainly not what people like us would go back to if we let ourselves," Siobhan told her.

"I just want everything to go away," Keoghan murmured.

"You can't do that by opening your veins to whatever you put inside them. I've learned that."

"How long have you been here?"

Siobhan sighed. "A few months. But I'm one of the extended stay patients. You should be out of here in two, tops."

"Do you really think I'll be able to do that?" Keoghan asked. "I'm... I don't know if I can."

"You have a fire in you, Keoghan. Mine had been put out, stomped on, and thrown into the Mariana Trench. Yours is almost dead, but I can see a tiny spark in it. You need to let that spark burn."

Keoghan nodded blankly. "Alright."

"I'm sorry," Siobhan laughed. "I'm... I get poetic sometimes. What I meant to say is, you want to live. I know you do. You want to live much more than many people who we see here do. Take advantage of that."

"Yeah. Thanks, Siobhan."

"No problem."

"Hey," Keoghan murmured as she climbed into her bed. "How many women here have eating disorders?"

Siobhan nodded, grimacing. "A lot of us. Why? Do you?"

Keoghan sighed. "Yeah. I do. I was supposed to be getting better, but then all this shit happened."

"The good old drug and disorder combo," Siobhan said sagely. "You don't have to recover to get out of here, but like I said earlier, you have to get comfortable with gaining weight."

"I don't know if I'll ever be able to do that."

"Then you have to just deal. Trust me, I fought back the first time I came here, and I ended up getting tubed. I didn't even know they had those things here," Siobhan told her.

"Alright," Keoghan exhaled. "No tubes for me."

"Attagirl. Breakfast is at 8 tomorrow, and someone'll come in to wake us up if we aren't already up and at 'em. Good luck."

Keoghan nodded. "Yeah. I'm going to try to sleep now, then. Goodnight, Siobhan."

"Goodnight, Keoghan."

As she drifted into sleep, Keoghan heard Siobhan continue to sing to herself.

"You're scaring us, and all of us, some of us love you, Achilles, it's not much but it's proof."

31

The next day, Keoghan met Soledad over telehealth. She sat in front of the clinic's computer wringing her hands. What if Soledad was upset at her for disappearing? For using? For cutting?

"Hello, Keoghan," a warm voice spoke from the computer. "It's nice seeing you again, though I wish it were under different conditions."

Keoghan looked at the screen sheepishly. "Yeah. Hi, Soledad."

"Tell me about what your life has been like since we last spoke in January," she said gently. "Anything you feel comfortable sharing is what I want to know."

Nodding, Keoghan began to tell her everything. How Balthy had attacked her. How she ran away. How Finch found her. How she lived with him and his ex, used with them, even slept with them. How she lived in a self-harm and drugged haze, always doing what she could to avoid thinking about Stanford. How she got caught. How she was brought to the clinic. Soledad listened and nodded.

"Thank you," she told her. "You're very brave for telling me all of this. I'm glad you're getting help."

"I'll be coming back home soon," Keoghan asserted. "I promise."

"Don't rush it. I, and everyone else, would prefer you're there for a few more weeks than have you come back and relapse."

Keoghan nodded. "Yeah. I know."

"Tell me about Finch and his ex... Erica? Let me check my notes-Erica. How were they?"

"Well..." Keoghan told Soledad as much as she knew. Erica had still loved Finch, but he had resentment toward her. He always wanted her to use more, use with him and Keoghan, despite her reservations.

Keoghan admired Erica for standing strong, but she often wondered why Erica loved him. Sure, she liked him, but he was an asshole. Eventually, though, she gave in.

The words came spilling out of her as she felt relief from all the burdens she'd been carrying. There was something freeing about talking to someone, even if it was about topics she knew were taboo.

Perhaps that was the point of a therapist.

Keoghan's first session of group therapy took place later in the day. She sat next to Siobhan, who was doodling on a piece of paper, while they waited for the staff member in charge of overseeing the group to arrive.

"What are you drawing?" Keoghan asked quietly.

Siobhan slid the paper over so Keoghan could see. "My guitar. It's in my room, but I haven't played it in a while."

"Why's that?"

"Memories," Siobhan sighed. "Do you have things like that? Something you love, maybe more than anything else, that was tainted by memories?"

Keoghan nodded. Her coffee order. Halloween. Her dorm room. Stanford itself.

"Yeah. A couple."

"So you get it."

"I do. But..."

Siobhan gave her a half-smile. "But?"

"You should play again. Reclaim the memories," Keoghan told her. "I'd love to hear it."

Nodding slowly, Siobhan drew spirals on her paper around the instrument. "Yeah. Maybe I will."

One morning- Keoghan had lost track of time- Keoghan and the other women sat in the common area when the same woman who brought her in came with a familiar face.

"Ladies, this is-"

"Erica?" Keoghan exclaimed.

The woman was gaunt, shaking with clouded eyes.

Erica nodded. "Hi, Sunnie."

"Erica, I'll bring your bags to your room. You'll be just down the hall, sharing with Reb. I'll leave you to talk to Keoghan and the others."

Erica slowly walked over to where the other women sat. "Is Keoghan your real name?"

"Yeah," Keoghan responded. "What are you doing here?"

"Who is this?" Siobhan asked. "Sorry. That seemed rude. Did you know each other from... this?"

"I'm Keoghan's part-time-boyfriend Finch's ex-girlfriend. We all lived together and, uh, shot up together."

Siobhan nodded. "Damn. What happened to Finch, then?"

"He..." Erica sniffed, wiping her eyes. "He died. Someone put fent in his..."

Keoghan felt like someone had struck her with lightning. Finch. He had always seemed like the strongest man on the planet, unable to die no matter how much he used.

"Fuck," she whispered. "Finch is dead..."

Erica sighed. "Maybe it's for the better. He was so suicidal, you know, if he hadn't gone out with fear in his eyes I would have thought he did it himself."

"Yeah..."

The room went quiet, a moment of remembrance and gratefulness. Finch and Erica had been constants in Keoghan's life since she met them, and to have one gone and another about to be changed massively... it would be a difficult road.

"How's the withdrawal?" Erica asked. "Is it bad?"

Keoghan nodded. She had been anxious to no end, her heart had begun to race, she could barely keep any food down, and the desire to use had been all-consuming. The pain was unbearable, not just physical pain, but emotional. William, Lukas, Eri, and now Finch weighed heavily on her mind. She wanted to carve into her skin, to numb the thoughts with as much physical pain as she could handle. It was all too much.

Siobhan seemed to notice that she was retreating into a dark space again and gave her a smile. "It'll get better, Keoghan… and Erica."

"Yeah," Keoghan mumbled. "It'll get better."

Erica's eyes remained on the floor, but she nodded.

"Erica, let me give you the rundown on this lovely little part of Sunnyvale," Siobhan began, launching into a speech that Keoghan tuned out.

Nobody was safe.

Everybody was going to die.

"Alright, ladies, welcome to your Skills Group of the day," a chipper staff member chirped later in the day. "For Erica, since she's new, Skills Group is a daily meeting where we discuss different therapeutic skills to aid your recovery. Today, we'll be reviewing a DBT skill in the distress tolerance module."

"Ooh, let me guess," Siobhan cried. "IMPROVE the moment!"

The woman nodded with a laugh. "How many times have you learned this skill, Siobhan?"

"Only, you know, six times."

"Well, it's one of my favorites. Okay, I have some handouts for you…"

Keoghan looked over at Erica, who was white-knuckling the chair she sat on. She wondered if everything was a blur for her, if she also had a song playing in her head, if she had someone who would kiss her and pick her up and keep her safe.

Probably not.

Hopefully she would be taken care of. If by nobody else, by Keoghan. She would have a home where she could recover. If nobody else gave it to her, Keoghan would. She would have someone to support her. If nobody else did, Keoghan would.

Keoghan would.

32

Life in the clinic was very monotonous. Wake up, eat breakfast, group therapy, individual therapy with Soledad, eat lunch, Skills Group, free time, eat dinner. Keoghan was adjusting to her new routine, and it seemed like Erica was as well. Siobhan brought humor and light into their days, and Reb conversed softly with Alyssa and Mickie, who had begun to speak. Erica began to crack open, revealing the sunshine Keoghan knew her by.

Keoghan's phone privileges were been restored, and she texted her friends daily. Every other day, she video called Iris, and her friends made an effort to appear in the frame.

"You gonna call your girlfriend again tonight?" Siobhan asked about a month into Keoghan's stay. "She's so nice."

Keoghan nodded. "Yeah. She really is. She was the one that dropped me off here."

"Was she also the one that found you?"

"No. That was Celena, the redhead who swears a lot. You'll recognize her as soon as you meet her," Keoghan smiled. "I can't wait to see all of them."

Her phone rang as soon as she finished speaking, and she opened the video call.

"KAY!" Celena shouted so loudly that the phone's speaker cut out. "Show me your cool roommate! Iris told me about her."

"Siobhan, want to meet Celena?"

"Sure," Siobhan laughed, sitting down next to Keoghan. "Hi, Celena."

"Oh my god, you're so fucking cool. I love your hair. And you're wearing a Limp Bizkit shirt. I love Limp Bizkit!"

Nodding, Siobhan reached into the pocket of her cargo pants and pulled out an old iPod. "I have a lot of their music, and that of artists like them, on here. When I didn't have phone permissions, I'd listen to it with a shitty pair of wired earbuds. I still do it now, just with a better pair of headphones."

"Dude! I love that!" Celena cried. "Jesus fuck, you're like... amazing."

"You wanna see something even cooler?"

Celena's eyes shone. "Yes!"

Siobhan walked over to her clothes, piled on the floor yet folded, and pulled out an old t-shirt. She brought it over to the two women and held it up.

"Constella Will Make You Come (back for more)," Celena read. "What's Constella?"

"My old band," Siobhan told her. "I was the vocalist and guitarist."

"Holy shit, dude, you're so cool," Celena whispered, getting a determined look in her eyes.

Iris took the phone back and smiled at Keoghan. "Hey, Keoghan. I had to take the phone away from Celena before she made plans to bust you two out. How are you?"

"I'm well," Keoghan responded. "I get to go out on a trip to get ice cream tomorrow."

After patients were deemed well enough, they were allowed to go on weekly staffed group excursions. Keoghan had been psychologically well enough for the last excursion, but her withdrawals were keeping her mostly bedbound. Finally, three days prior, she had been able to attend enough groups to earn her freedom.

"That's awesome," Iris smiled. "Any word on your discharge date?"

"May 10th," Keoghan responded. "I found out earlier today."

"That's in... one month. Oh, Keoghan, I'm so proud of you."

"Thank you. I'm so excited to see you and everyone else again."

Siobhan kicked Keoghan's foot with her own. "Gonna miss you. But it's a good thing. We all gotta get out of here and never come back."

Keoghan nodded. "Yeah. Do you know when you're being discharged?"

"Sometime in July, maybe," Siobhan sighed. "I don't know. But I'm happy for you. And your girlfriend, of course."

Iris offered Siobhan a small smile. "You'll make it. Keoghan and I have the utmost amount of faith in you."

"Thanks, Iris. I just have to keep holding on this time. It's my second time in rehab," Siobhan admitted. "Same clinic, too. That's why they're keeping me for longer this time."

Keoghan kicked Siobhan's foot back. "You told me I have a fire in me. Well, I can see yours. It's coming back, Siobhan. What did you tell me? You need to-"

"Harness it. Take advantage of it," Siobhan said. "Yeah. I need to make sure nobody throws my fire into the Trench again."

"Exactly. And I gave you my number and Instagram a few days ago. Talk to me whenever you need."

"Thanks, Keoghan."

Keoghan nodded. "Of course."

Iris's phone was ripped out of her hands, and Celena's face took up the entire screen. "KAY! IRIS SAID YOU'RE GETTING DISCHARGED IN A MONTH- OH MY GOD, FUCK YEAH, I LOVE YOU SO MUCH!"

Smiling, Keoghan nodded. "Yeah. I'll see you soon, Celena."

"You better. We're going to throw you a party at our new place, Iris and I found one that we put a deposit on. It's such a cute apartment, and you're going to fucking love it."

"I'm sure I will. I can't wait."

"Oh, shit, I have to go. Bye, Kay! I'll talk to you soon. Bye, Siobhan!" Celena told them, waving and handing the phone back to Iris. "Byeeeeeeeee!"

Keoghan laughed. "It's going to be so nice to see you guys again in person."

"Dinner time, ladies!" a voice called.

"I guess you have to go?" Iris asked.

"Yeah. I'll talk to you soon. I love you."

"I love you too, Keoghan. Talk to you soon."

Iris hung up, and Keoghan walked to the dining room with the other women.

"How much weight have you gained?" Erica whispered as they waited for the door to open.

Keoghan grimaced. "Fifteen pounds."

"Jesus," Erica sighed. "And I know you have your whole anorexia thing..."

"Yeah. I... It's insane."

"How are you feeling?"

"I don't... I don't know. It's a mindfuck."

Erica nodded. "Mindfuck indeed."

"It's, like... it's getting better," Keoghan told her. "I'm getting used to it. I hate it, of course, but... it's..."

"Yeah. It'll get better soon."

Keoghan and Erica sat on the floor of Keoghan's room, watching Siobhan tune her guitar as she sat on the bed.

"Alright," Siobhan sighed. "I got it."

"Rock our shit," Erica smiled.

Siobhan began to strum the strings of the black, stick-on-jewel covered electric guitar. "God, this is so much better with a pick."

Still, music flowed through the room. Keoghan tapped her fingers against the ground as the song picked up.

"*I drove my car off the bridge listening to Radio City, when our song came on, the one you used to sing with me...*" Siobhan sang gently.

"I know this song!" Erica cried. "*Fuck it, I can't drive, but I'd like to imagine.*"

"Put my hurt in a scene and then see what happens." Siobhan laughed quietly as Erica closed her eyes and sang with her.

"Take it from me, I'm not looking for anybody, take it from me..."

Erica shifted herself over to sit next to Siobhan's leg and leaned against it.

"I'm sick of car rides, you lied while we lay back to side. Now I'm driving and I hear you singing about how you got high, got high, got high..."

Keoghan smiled. She didn't know the song, but Siobhan and Erica were swaying and singing as Siobhan strummed the chords out. It was beautiful, exactly what she had hoped Siobhan would experience.

"Wanna start smoking just to feel the rush, I liked someone who did it once, I wanna get off this road I'm on but I'm stuck at the wheel..."

"You're such a good singer," Siobhan murmured as Erica took a breath in.

Erica smiled, her eyes sparkling, and kept singing. *"Take it from me, I'm not looking for anybody, take it from me..."*

When the song ended, Keoghan felt she had walked in on an intimate moment between Siobhan and Erica. The music they had created moved her deeply, and it imbued her with the knowledge that things would get better.

Things would be okay.

A few days later, Keoghan sat in the kitchen with Reb, Erica, and Siobhan, eating the rest of the clinic's Easter food. She had made peace with the fact that to leave, she had to restore enough weight to be "healthy". Still, she knew her newfound freedom around food would be temporary. The moment someone else died- and she knew someone would- things would come crashing down. She just knew it.

"I think I'm going to vomit if I ever have to see another Peep," Siobhan laughed, ripping the head off of one of the marshmallow rabbits. "I've eaten more of those things here than I have in years."

"I only saw them in stores," Keoghan commented. "My mother was... what do people say on the internet? Almond mom?"

Erica nodded. "Fuck her, dude. Almond moms are horrible."

Keoghan grabbed a sausage roll and wiggled it across Siobhan's vision with an evil smirk on her face. "Don't you want one of these?"

"Get it away!" Siobhan cried. "God, no more. Do you know how many sausage rolls I ate on Easter? I don't even celebrate Easter!"

"They're so good, though," Erica laughed, taking one and holding it directly in front of Siobhan.

Reb smiled and joined in. "Oooooo, sausage roll..."

"No more, I say! Leave me in peace!"

Keoghan stuffed the sausage roll into her mouth. "Erica, isn't your birthday soon?"

"Oh, right," Erica sighed. "I forgot age was a thing. Yeah, I'm turning twenty-two."

"Jesus, you're old. I'm nineteen in July."

"We're all old when we're in rehab," Sioban said sagely. "I'm twenty-two already."

"I'm twenty-three," Reb added.

"God, I'm surrounded by old spinsters..." Keoghan joked.

"Just because *you* have a girlfriend doesn't mean we're spinsters," Erica told her. "We have each other, which is... close enough."

"You'll never pass as my spinster girlfriend if you don't dye that hair," Siobhan laughed. "What do you think, Keoghan? Blue?"

"Hell yeah, blue. Erica, we're buying you hair dye," Keoghan decided. "I need to re-do my hair, but I'll wait a bit to decide on the color."

"Help, staff, I'm getting peer-pressured," Erica giggled. "Fine. Let's do this."

"Don't touch my hair," Reb laughed. "I worked hard to stop it from falling out."

"Don't worry, you're too old for me," Siobhan smiled.

33

Keoghan, Erica, and Siobhan sat in the hallway that contained everyone's rooms. Reb, Alyssa, and Mickie were in the common area, preparing a secret birthday celebration for Erica. It was Keoghan and Siobhan's job to keep her distracted. Erica stared at Siobhan's hair, which had gained a pink streak in her bangs. Her own hair had been dyed blue at the same time, with some pink in it as well.

"Erica, how was your first excursion?" Siobhan asked. Erica had been cleared for excursions the week prior.

"It was fun," Erica smiled. Keoghan noticed that over her time in the clinic, Erica had gotten happier. She had always been a ray of sunshine in Keoghan and Finch's clouded lives, but now she was learning to live and be truly happy. The excursion, a trip to a local boba shop, had brightened her as well.

"I really enjoyed the tea I got," she continued. "The pomegranate flavor was really good. Sun- er, Keoghan, did you like your tea? It was kumquat, right?"

Keoghan nodded. "It was also good. They had little mango jellies in there, and that was the best part."

"Oh, that sounds amazing..."

Reb walked into the hallway and grinned. "Alright, you can come in now. Erica, close your eyes."

She did, and Siobhan led her into the common space, Keoghan close behind.

"Ready?" Siobhan called. "One, two, Erica, open your eyes!"

"*Happy birthday to you,*" everyone began to sing. "*Happy birthday to you. Happy birthday, dear Erica... Happy birthday to you!*"

"Oh my God, thank you guys so much!" Erica cried. "You totally didn't have to do this... thank you!"

Keoghan looked around the room. A handmade banner was hung on the windowed wall, proclaiming "ERICA IS OLD NOW", balloons were tied to the chairs and table legs, handmade garland was everywhere, and a plate with six small cupcakes stood on the table in the center of the room.

Erica ran around, hugging each person in turn.

"Thank you, Reb! Thank you, Alyssa! Mickie, thank you! Keoghan... Sunnie... thank you! And Siobhan," Erica paused, smiling widely at the woman and taking her hand, "thank you!"

"Of course, Chay," Siobhan told her, wrapping her into a tight hug. "It's not just your twenty-second birthday, it's also your first as part of the rehab family."

"And the queers with colored hair," Erica giggled. "Keoghan, get in here."

Keoghan laughed and held Erica close. "Us bi girls have to stick together, huh?"

"Don't forget your lesbian leader," Siobhan smiled. "Reb, Mickie, and Alyssa are our underlings."

Mickie smiled, the first time Keoghan had seen her do it since she arrived. "If I'm pan, am I still an underling?"

"No, you're part of the elite council."

The group bantered about power structures as they ate their cupcakes, allowing themselves to be something that they usually couldn't: bare. Open. Free.

Together.

Erica's discharge date was announced the next day. She would be leaving at the same time as Siobhan- July 2nd. Keoghan's birthday.

A few days later, Reb was discharged. Alyssa and Mickie spent a long time in conversation with her before she left, and the other three women sent her off with a goodbye and a hug. Keoghan regretted not being closer with her, but she wouldn't give up her friendship with Erica and Siobhan for the off chance of making a connection. Reb had still been kind and warm, so Keoghan wanted the best for her.

A week passed, and Keoghan's time came. She woke up at 5AM on May 10th, much earlier than usual, and set about beginning to gather her things. Her chargers for her phone and earbuds, the decorations she had put up in her room, her assortment of toiletries, everything went into her bags. There were many things she hadn't even gotten out but had just brought with her to spare them from gathering dust in room 306.

"Keoghan?" Siobhan mumbled, sitting up and rubbing her eyes. "Oh, shit. You're leaving today."

Keoghan nodded. "Yeah. I am."

"Okay, since you're leaving in, like, two and a half hours... can I tell you a secret?" Siobhan asked, motioning for Keoghan to come closer.

Walking across the room, Keoghan nodded. "I'd love to hear."

"Me 'n Erica? We're gonna get a place together once we get out of here. We're gonna live in Half-Moon Bay."

Keoghan smiled. "That's great, Siobhan. Neither of you will be alone anymore."

"Yeah," Siobhan sighed happily. "It's the first time I haven't been alone since, Jesus, Junior year of high school. Before the drugs, or, well, before they got bad. I was in a band then, and my bandmates all died or moved away. No matter how many people we replaced them with, I was the only one left by the time I graduated. I thought I was cursed, y'know? So I started using more, cutting more, eating less... the whole thing. Before I knew it, I was waking up in strangers' houses with marks or tattoos on me that I never remembered getting. I lost contact with every good person I knew, except one. My sister, who lived all the way in Missouri, called me one day and told me if I didn't get my ass into rehab, she wouldn't call me anymore. So I went to rehab. Got out. My sister died at the hands of her ex-boyfriend. I relapsed, and I thought there was nobody there to save me like she did. I didn't want to be saved by anyone else. Then one day, I was with my girlfriend at the time, we were doing our thing, and she just... died. Right there, right in front of me. We didn't have the money for an ambulance, but I called one anyway. They said she OD'd. They also told me that if I wanted to avoid getting repercussions for the drugs, I had to go into rehab. Again. So..."

"So you came back," Keoghan murmured. "I'm so proud of you for that, Siobhan."

"I can't afford to come back here a third time, literally. Neither can Erica. So we're going to stick together."

Keoghan nodded. Erica would be taken care of. There was nobody in the world that she would trust her with more than Siobhan. They would both be alright. She knew it.

"Keoghan?"

"Yeah?"

"Don't lose contact with me. I love you like a sister, and I want you to stick around," Siobhan told her.

Smiling, Keoghan pulled Siobhan into a hug. "I want you to stick around too... big sis."

"God, that makes me feel old."

"Well, you are."

Siobhan laughed gently and pushed aside her blankets. "Alright. Let's rock this shit."

34

Siobhan and Erica insisted on walking Keoghan out as far as they were allowed to go. Once their staff member told them they couldn't go further, they took turns hugging her.

"Visit us," Erica told her. "Sio'll send you the address."

Keothan nodded. "I will. I can't wait to see you again once we're out of there."

Siobhan squeezed her so tight that Keoghan thought she would combust. "Chay and I will hold down the fort. You just focus on making sure we don't see you back here before we leave, alright?"

"Yeah," Keoghan smiled. "I'll see you soon, but not here."

"Not here!" the two women chorused.

"Alright, let's give Keoghan her space so she can prepare to leave. Keoghan, is there anything you could have forgotten? Anything you need?" the staff member asked.

Keoghan shook her head. "I have everything."

"Okay. Are you ready?"

"Yes."

The staff member opened the door leading out to the lobby, and Keoghan stepped out of the clinic.

She was free.

"KAY!" she heard Celena scream, followed by thundering footsteps. "Oh my God, Kay! You're here!"

A force that could only be described as a bolt of Celena hit her, and she nearly toppled over as her friend hugged her and lifted her off the ground.

"Hey, Celena," Keoghan greeted. "I missed you."

"I missed you more. Come on, Iris is waiting with everyone else," Celena told her. "Oh, and… I quit vaping. In solidarity."

"I'm glad," Keoghan smiled.

She followed Celena to where her friends waited. Iris, Chloe, and Elizabeth stood near the entrance to the building, and as soon as Keoghan approached they ran to her.

"Keoghan!" Chloe called. "You're here!"

"I am," Keoghan laughed. "I'm free."

"Congratulations, Keoghan," Elizabeth smiled. "Your 'boyfriend' is so proud of you."

"Thank you-" Keoghan cut herself off as she saw tears begin to fall down Iris's cheeks. "Are you okay?"

"I'm so happy, Keoghan," Iris sobbed. "I'm so fucking happy."

Iris pulled Keoghan in and kissed her. Keoghan melted into her, wrapping her arms around her girlfriend's body. This was good. This was… love.

"That's gay," Chloe joked. "Filthy queers."

Iris shook her head and pressed her forehead against Keoghan's.

"No, this is totally platonic," she deadpanned.

"This is the epitome of friendship," Keoghan giggled. "I'm so happy to see all of you again."

Celena smiled and nodded. "Let's get out of here. We need to show you our new place!"

Keoghan gasped. "You have it already?"

"Hell yeah we do. Come on!"

As the group left the clinic carrying Keoghan's bags, it felt as though she was being reborn. She had been beaten to death by her own trauma, but she was reemerging. She was making a new life for herself, one step at a time.

ACT SIX: NEW GROWTH

35

The drive to the new apartment was filled with chatter and music, everyone taking turns choosing songs to play. Keoghan sat in the "seat of honor," as Celena called it, known to everyone else as the passenger seat.

They arrived at the apartment, a short bike ride away from campus, and pulled into their designated parking spot.

"Chloe and Elizabeth chose to live on-campus for one more year," Celena explained. "So this apartment is just for you, me, and Iris."

Iris unlocked the door and motioned Keoghan in. She entered and looked around. There were boxes in every room.

"We'll look for furniture on some buy-nothing groups," Iris told her.

Keoghan nodded. "Sounds good."

"Do you want me to take a picture of you guys in here?" Chloe asked. "Something to remember today by?"

"Hell yeah," Celena cried. "Here, take my phone."

Celena slung her arms around Keoghan and Iris and pulled them close. Chloe snapped a few pictures. Keoghan hoped she didn't look fat in the pictures, remembering the amount of weight she had gained in the facility. She knew that in theory, she was dangling on the cusp of where she had to be to leave, but it was more than she'd weighed in years.

"It'll be sad to have to say goodbye to you two," she told Chloe and Elizabeth, attempting to push away those thoughts.

"One day, we're all gonna live together in a giant house and we'll never have to say goodbye again," Celena said.

Elizabeth nodded. "That would be amazing."

"Are you guys sure you're okay with living on campus?" Keoghan asked.

"Yeah," Chloe smiled. "I don't want to have to drive or bike to my classes."

"Alright. If you need to stay somewhere, we'll find a couch for you."

"We better have a couch regardless," Celena laughed.

"I did find a nice one on the buy-nothing group," Iris told her. "Want me to put in a request for it?"

"Hell yeah."

Iris sent a message to the owner of the couch, and the women walked around the apartment. Keoghan and Iris would be sharing a room, and Celena would have one next to it. They sat on the floor of the living room and looked at furniture to send requests for, laughing and talking.

Keoghan felt alive with her friends. She felt whole. There was nothing that could bring her down anymore... as long as she stayed small. As long as Iris still loved her. As long as nobody else died. As long as nothing bad happened to her ever again. Deep down, she knew she was still fragile. Her experiences may have hardened her, but reinforced glass still breaks.

The next day, Keoghan went to see Soledad. She had stayed in Iris's dorm for the night, and while she was at therapy Iris would pick up the couch for her to sleep on the next night.

The office hadn't changed at all in the months since she had last seen it. Still decorated in monochromatic pastel hues, she felt a strange sense of comfort in the lack of change. She hadn't been away that long. Everything would be exactly how she left it.

"Keoghan?" Soledad called, stepping into the waiting room. "It's nice to see you again in person."

Keoghan smiled and stood up. "Yeah. It's nice to be back."

They ascended the stairs into Soledad's office, which hadn't changed either. When the two women sat down, Soledad gave Keoghan a reassuring smile.

"How are you feeling?"

"I'm... I'm alright," Keoghan responded.

Soledad nodded knowingly. "Alright as in good, or alright as in surviving?"

"Both? I'm doing well, but I also know I could break at any point. I know it wouldn't take much for me to fall down and shatter."

"Is this a new feeling, or have you been experiencing it in the clinic as well?"

Keoghan thought about it. In the clinic, she was wrapped in bubble wrap. She was sheltered and controlled so much that even the good couldn't truly get to her. Now, she was free- but unshielded.

"It's new, but I don't hate it," she said eventually. "I know that I have to learn to live with it."

Soledad nodded again. "Sometimes, the hard things are the most important catalysts in shaping who we are."

"Yeah," Keoghan sighed, reflecting on Soledad's words. What had shaped who she was? William's assault set off the series of events in her past year. Lukas's suicide led her to accept her queerness. Eri's death brought her closer to her friends. Balthy's attack drove her to using, which sent her to rehab, which let her meet some of the strongest people she knew. Looking back even further, her mother's abuse had given her an eating disorder. Her father's absence had led her to crave attention.

"I think I need to stop thinking," Keoghan murmured, shaking her head.

"Let's go over a skill for that, then. A DBT skill, because, if you couldn't tell, they're my favorites," Soledad smiled.

Keoghan crossed her legs in the chair. "Alright."

That night, Keoghan began her job search. Her previous employer had fired her after she didn't show up, a decision she knew was right but made life endlessly more difficult for her. She applied to any place that would take her. It was one thing to leech off of her parents, but they had refused to help her move out of the dorms because "she was just going to use the money to buy drugs". Their words stung, as Keoghan had never asked them for money during her addiction, and she had hoped that they could still see her as the same person as she was before. She refused to ask her friends to pay her portion of rent for longer than necessary. They had already done so much for her, she couldn't ask them for more.

Right as she was about to close her laptop for the night, her eyes landed on one job: a barista at the coffee shop she had met William at.

Feeling a rush of courage, Keoghan opened the application.

A few days later, Keoghan received an interview request from the coffee shop. She steeled her nerves, slung her purse over her shoulder, and walked to her bicycle.

It was time to reclaim herself.

When she arrived at the coffee shop, she was immediately hit with memories. William, standing at the counter. William, taking her to the back room. William, shooting himself. She dug her self-defense keychain into her palm, and she felt the blood thundering through her veins. It had to go away. Everything had to go away. She needed it to go away.

"Keoghan Winchester?" a friendly voice asked, piercing through Keoghan's thoughts. "Hi. I'm Alex, and I'll be interviewing you."

Keoghan smiled at Alex. They were short, with neon-pink hair and almost every piercing Keoghan could think of. Motioning for her to go behind the counter, Keoghan followed them into the back room.

"Don't think you can escape me, almond milk bi-"

Keoghan punched William directly in the jugular. He would not be coming for her again. She would not let him.

Alex pulled a chair out for her, and she sat down.

"Thank you for having me, Alex," she smiled at them.

"Of course! We love having students work here, especially ones who live off-campus. So, your name is Keoghan Sonata Winchester..."

Half an hour later, Keoghan was told that they would "consider her application as a formality, but hire her".

Keoghan began working a week after the interview. Every time she walked into the coffee shop, William made an appearance, but his voice was getting quieter. Weaker. He went from threatening to begging, laughing to sobbing. Keoghan knew that soon, he would be gone entirely.

Alex worked with her most days, and she enjoyed their company. When there were lulls in the wave of customers, they sat behind the counter and chatted.

"Are you planning on doing anything else with your hair?" Alex asked. "Your roots are really grown in. Not in a bad way, it's cool, but I know it's not usually everyone's ideal look."

Keoghan lifted a strand of her hair and shrugged. "I kind of want to cut it off."

"I have a friend who does hair. I can take you to them, if you want."

"Really?" Keoghan asked, slightly wary. "Do you have pictures of their work?"

Alex nodded and pulled out their phone. "Here's their Instagram page."

Scrolling through the page, Keoghan nodded. The work was good, and it seemed legitimate. They seemed to work with all different types of hair, and each cut suited the client well. She lingered on a picture of someone with bright green hair, someone who looked just like Siobhan, and again on a woman with Erica's shaggy blue hair.

"Alright. I'll go."

A few days passed, but Alex went through with their word. Keoghan found herself in a small salon, sitting in a chair in front of Alex's friend Sasha. They were tall, with buzzed hair in a leopard print pattern.

"You have great hair," they told her. "Alex said you want to cut it off?"

"Not all of it. Just... a lot. And I want to re-do the color of my bangs, but I can do it at home," she responded.

"No. I can tell you've been through some shit- hair holds memories and trauma. That's why I cut mine off. Here's the deal: I'm going to give you the best treatment you can get, and I'm not going to ask for payment, alright? If you like it, consider the payment to be coming back."

Keoghan smiled, slightly unsure. "Are you sure? I can definitely pay-"

"Damn sure. Consider it a favor amongst friends. Come on, let's get your hair washed."

When they stood in front of the mirror again, Sasha held Keoghan's hair up. "How short are we thinking?"

"Just above shoulder-length, but with shorter bangs."

"Sounds good. And what colors for the bangs?"

"I think... green. With some blue streaks," Keoghan decided.

"That's fucking awesome. Any reason for that, or just for fun?" Sasha asked.

"Well, I met some friends in, uh, rehab. One of them had green and pink hair, and the other had blue and pink hair. I know they did the pink to match each other, so I'll just take the green and pink from them."

Sasha smiled. "Amazing. You meet the best people in places like that. I remember my medical center led me to meeting some of my closest friends."

"Yeah," Keoghan nodded, curious about Sasha's medical treatment. "You do."

A few hours later, Keoghan had a massive weight lifted off her shoulders- literally. Her hair was much shorter, and her bangs were bright again. It felt like a fresh start.

"Before you go," Sasha told her as they toweled off her hair, "I want to tell you a story of mine."

Keoghan smiled. "Go ahead."

"When I was fourteen, I was in a really bad place. I was the only non-binary person I knew, and my family was Russian Orthodox, so you know how they felt. Well, a lot of shit happened, and I ended up in the hospital for an eating disorder and an overdose. My parents refused to let me get mental treatment, so I was kept in the eating disorder ward of the hospital. I celebrated my fifteenth birthday in the hospital. When I was released, my parents told me that if I lost any more weight I'd be on my own, so I tried to maintain my weight. Eventually, I earned some semblance of trust back, but I was never the same. I secretly tried to overdose no less than five separate times after I was released. Eventually, I ended up in the adult psych ward. But my point of this story is: everything that happened to me led me here. I learned to cut and dye hair after I was fired from my job for taking too much time off for my psych ward stay. I started working on my own, without a license, and eventually saved up enough money to get one. All the things that happened to you, all the assault and mental shit... you're going to go far, Keoghan. You're going to go really far."

Nodding, Keoghan's eyes began to sparkle. "Thank you, Sasha."

"Of course. Do come back sometime, even when you're not here for an appointment. I'd love to talk more."

"Do you want my Instagram, then? I'd love to stay in contact with you and, you know, come back for my hair.."

Sasha nodded. "I'd love that. There's a connection here, one between souls."

"I think the same," Keoghan smiled, pulling out her phone. "Alright. My username's keothejester..."

<h1 style="text-align:center">36</h1>

June.

Why did Keoghan like June? It wasn't because school ended, as that usually meant she would have to go home. It wasn't because of Pride, as she had never attended any sort of event. She couldn't think of any reason to like June, but she did anyway.

Iris and Celena officially moved into their apartment as soon as the semester ended, and Keoghan immediately felt less alone. It had been difficult for her to live alone, to keep her promises to stay clean and sober without someone watching her, but she managed to claw her way to the finish line.

Work had been a good escape. Alex was great, and they had even taken her to get her first piercing (a gold nostril ring) a few days prior to Iris and Celena's move-in date. After a while, Keoghan even opened up to them about William and the events that had taken place in the very place they worked.

"Jesus, Keoghan," Alex sighed. "I'm so sorry. I worked here when William did, and I can tell you that it was in no way your fault. He liked to call abuser on people who he abused, and claimed to be traumatized from a woman telling him no. You did nothing wrong."

Keoghan nodded. "Thank you. I'm... I'm coming to terms with what happened. I think everything is going to work out."

"It will. You deserve it to work out."

Keoghan and Sasha talked frequently, sharing stories of their lives and sending each other stupid reels. They lived too far apart to see one another regularly, but both agreed to make the commute to Sasha's shop at least once a month.

Elizabeth stopped by Keoghan's apartment one day with a devilish grin.

"Chloe's in the car," she told Keoghan as soon as the door was opened. "You're coming with us. Iris and Celena will meet us where we're going."

Keoghan nodded slowly and picked up her shoes. "Where exactly are we going?"

"You'll see."

After her shoes were on, Keoghan followed Elizabeth to her car. When she sat down, Chloe handed her a small package.

"You'll be needing that," she smiled. "Open it when we get there."

"What the hell is going on?" Keoghan laughed. "Are you kidnapping me?"

"Yes."

Elizabeth drove them to a park close to the apartment where several tents were set up around a stage. People were milling about, and the parking lot was nearly completely full. They eventually found a spot to park and exited the car. Keoghan opened the package that Chloe had given her.

"A... bisexual pride flag?"

"Welcome to your first Pride, Kay!"

Keoghan looked up. Celena was standing in front of her, smiling broadly. A lesbian flag was tied around her neck. Iris stood close behind, a small trans flag drawn on her face.

"You kidnapped me to take me to Pride?" Keoghan laughed. "Oh my God."

"Come on! The drag show is about to start," Celena told her, grabbing her wrist. "And put your flag on."

"How?" Keoghan asked.

Iris stepped behind her. "May I?"

Keoghan nodded. Iris took the flag and gently tied two ends together around Keoghan's neck, her fingers causing the feeling of sparks whenever she brushed her skin. Keoghan leaned her head backward to bump it against her.

"Thank you, Iris," she murmured.

Iris kissed her forehead gently. "Of course."

"Come on!" Celena groaned. "You can be gay while we're watching the show."

Keoghan laughed and began to walk. "Alright. Let's go."

They made their way to the stage, where a loud pop song was playing. A drag queen strutted down the stage to the beat. She had red hair that was shaved on one side with black tips, and she wore a bandage-like top with a black leather jacket and pants, accented by layers of studded belts and studded platform shoes.

"She's like Vi from Arcane," Iris gasped. "The pitfighter look, at least."

"I'm just livin' that life, Von Dutch, cult classic but I still pop. I get money, you get mad that the bank's shut..."

She reached the end and blew a kiss to the crowd, shimmying her shoulders and letting her leather jacket slide down her arms. Keoghan watched as she began to bend backwards, leaning her knees forward and arching her back.

"It's so obvious, I'm your number one, I'm your number one, I'm..."

She fell to the floor in a controlled motion and pushed herself back up, blowing another kiss. The music began to fade, and she strutted back to the top of the stage.

"Vi Agera, everybody!" a drag king shouted from the side of the stage.

"I knew it!" Iris laughed. "I want to see some of her other looks."

Keoghan smiled, watching as the next queen entered the stage. Drag seemed like such a unique way to express oneself. Why had her parents always spoken about the 'filthy drag queers'? In the end, they were just people. People like her, who needed a way to make themselves heard.

"Maybe Kay should try drag," she heard Celena joke. "She's absolutely transfixed on the show."

Keoghan nodded. "Maybe I should."

Long after the show was over, Keoghan's mind was still on the queens and kings she saw. They looked so happy and confident.

Drag. She'd remember that.

"Alright, Kay, can you hand me the Command hooks?" Celena asked, standing on top of her new bed. She was attempting to hang her lesbian flag from Pride above it, and was struggling to hold it in place.

"These ones?" Keoghan responded, picking up a package of white hooks.

"Yeah, those."

Keoghan peeled the back off of the hooks and handed them to her, smiling. It was amazing, beyond any words, to have her friends in the same home as her. It was the first time she could call somewhere her home, and she hadn't even finished making it hers.

"Once you're done, Keoghan, can you come into our room to approve the plants?" Iris called.

"Of course!" Keoghan smiled. She and Iris had bought fake plants at IKEA and planned to put them throughout their room. Her favorite was a faux potted vine that Iris had placed to cascade down the side of a desk. The other plants were expertly placed.

"It looks so good," Keoghan told Iris, standing behind her and wrapping her arms around her waist. "You did a good job."

Iris tilted her head to brush her nose against Keoghan's cheek and laughed softly. "Thank you."

"Get a room," Celena shouted from the doorway. "Don't remind me how I don't have a girlfriend."

"You'll find someone," Keoghan told her. "Anyone would be lucky to have you."

Celena nodded. "I guess. I just feel like nobody wants an ace relationship these days. Everyone is all about sex and sex appeal."

"If a woman doesn't want you the way you are, she's not worth it," Iris chimed in.

"Yeah. I swear to God, though, if I get my Bachelor's while still being a bachelorette I'm going to die."

"Don't die."

"I'll try."

A few days later, Keoghan called Siobhan and Erica.

"I'm moved into my new place," she told them.

Erica smiled. "You have to show us around."

"I concur," Siobhan agreed. "I want to see your room."

Keoghan stood up from the couch and showed them around the house. The living room had a heather blue couch and two gray beanbags around a rickety white coffee table, a table with five chairs that the women ate at, and a sideboard with fake plants and books on it. Taking them through the kitchen, which was separated from the living room by a half-wall, Keoghan brought them into the hallway with the bed- and bathrooms.

"I'm not going into Celena's room or bathroom, but here's Iris and mine."

Her room was lit up by fairy lights, with a queen bed in the middle and two nightstands, one on either side. There was a closet built into the wall and a dresser next to it, and the room connected to a bathroom.

"You and your girlfriend are sharing?" Siobhan asked. "That's gay, Keoghan."

"Oh, wow, I never knew that," Keoghan deadpanned.

"I'm so happy that you're living with your friends," Erica smiled. "You deserve it."

"And you guys get out in, what, two weeks? I'll happily help you house-hunt in Half-Moon Bay."

"Thank you. We've been looking when we can, and the staff have been helping us. We should be able to get a place we found, we have just enough for the down payment," Siobhan told her.

"That's great!"

"We'll come to visit you, of course, provided my car still works," Erica said. "I think it will, it hasn't been *that* long."

Keoghan nodded. "It'll be great to see you in our natural habitat."

"Keoghan, my natural habitat is a basement rock show," Siobhan laughed. "But yeah. It will be good to see you outside of the clinic."

"I want to visit Finch's grave with you," Erica murmured.

"I would love to do that."

"We have to show him that things get better. People aren't all as shitty as we thought back then."

"There is *some* good in the world," Siobhan said. "Just not a lot."

"Hey, some is better than nothing," Erica responded, bumping Siobhan's side.

"I guess that's true."

"Is that Siobhan and Erica?" Iris called. "Let me see them!"

Keoghan walked over to Iris and angled the phone so she could see the other women.

"Hey," Iris greeted with a smile.

"If it isn't Girlfriend," Siobhan responded. "I hope you're taking good care of my woman?"

"I'm your woman, Sio," Erica laughed. "Keoghan's your sidechick."

Keoghan smiled and shook her head. "Jesus…"

"I take it you're doing well?" Iris asked. "And yeah, I'd say I'm doing a good job of taking care of her."

"Good. If I find out that it's otherwise, I'm kidnapping her and taking her to Half-Moon Bay with me," Siobhan told Iris.

"Noted."

The women chatted until Siobhan and Erica were called to a meal. Keoghan hung up with a warm feeling in her chest. She was surrounded by love, by good things. The world could be shitty, but at least she had people who cared about her.

"Keoghan?" Iris asked, pulling her closer and kissing her. "I love you."

Keoghan smiled and cradled Iris's face in her hands. "I love you, too."

37

"Happy birthday, dear Keoghan... happy birthday to you!"

Keoghan, Iris, Celena, Chloe, and Elizabeth stood in her living room, and she sat on the couch. An overly frosted cake was placed on the coffee table, and everyone wore party hats.

"You're 19 now, you old bitch!" Celena laughed, running over to hug her.

Smiling, Keoghan leaned into her. "Hey, you're not that much younger than me."

Iris snapped a picture. "When are Siobhan and Erica coming?"

The doorbell rang.

"Let us in! We want to see the birthday girl!" Siobhan's voice called.

Keoghan stood up and let the two women in. "You're free!"

"Damn right we are," Siobhan smiled. "We're going to our apartment as soon as we're done here."

"That's amazing. I'm so glad that you two managed to get a place."

"It was mainly Sio," Erica told her. "I didn't do much."

"Okay, that's a lie. You helped a lot."

The women stepped inside and took off their shoes before walking to the living room. Keoghan followed behind them. Everyone took turns hugging Siobhan and Erica and congratulating them on their release from the clinic.

"Is that a cake I see?" Siobhan asked.

Chloe nodded. "I baked it."

"Our kitchen is still a mess from that," Iris laughed.

"An artist needs her space," Chloe countered. "And I think it's going to be good."

"Only one way to find out!" Erica smiled.

Elizabeth emerged from the kitchen- Keoghan didn't even realize she had left- holding a knife. "Keoghan, do you want to do the honors?"

Keoghan nodded and cut the cake into eight pieces.

"We each get one," she explained. "And then there's one left... for Lukas and Eri."

Iris took her hand and gave her a gentle smile. "Good."

"And hopefully nobody else," Celena added.

"Let's pour them a glass," Siobhan told them, pulling a bottle of red wine out of her bag. "I know three of us aren't supposed to be drinking, but it's a special occasion. And they deserve a memorial."

Keoghan touched her locket and nodded. "We don't have wine glasses, so we'll have to use regular ones."

"Good with me."

Celena and Iris ran into the kitchen to grab glasses. As they did, Erica laid her eyes on Keoghan's small speaker.

"We should play music," she suggested.

"Alright," Keoghan responded, turning it on and connecting her phone. "What do we want?"

"Since this is a birthday-slash-memorial, let's play something for Lukas and Eri."

Keoghan knew exactly what to play.

"And I'd give up forever to touch you, 'cause I know that you feel me somehow. You're the closest to heaven that I'll ever be, and I don't want to go home right now..."

"Is that my namesake?" Iris laughed, coming out of the kitchen with glasses.

"You were named after this song?" Erica asked. "That's so cool."

"Actually... I named myself after this song," Iris exhaled. Keoghan sent her a look of encouragement. She was doing it. She was coming out. "I'm a trans woman."

Smiles lit up the room, and Iris was bombarded with hugs and encouragement.

"I'm so proud of you," Keoghan murmured when it was her turn to hold Iris. "You did it."

"Yeah. I did."

And I don't want the world to see me, 'cause I don't think that they'd understand. When everything's meant to be broken, I just want you to know who I am..."

"Wine time!" Celena cried. "I want my drink!"

"Settle down, youngster," Siobhan joked, pouring the drinks. "The first one is for the fallen."

When all the glasses had been poured, Keoghan closed her eyes and raised hers. "To Lukas. I'm sorry that I'm older than you now; your birthday was before mine. But I love you, and I hope you're having fun with whatever is up there. I hope you have a nice boyfriend and a golden retriever and a tortoiseshell cat. I hope you... I hope you think of me. And I'll see you again someday, but not now. Reg and the Jester forever. And to Eri. You deserved so much better."

The room grew heavy as the silence consumed them.

"We love you, Eri," Chloe whispered. "We love you so much. We miss you. We... We really want you back."

"Cheers to that..." Celena said, the quietest Keoghan thought she'd ever heard her.

"When everything feels like the movies, yeah, you bleed just to know you're alive..."

"And we love you, too, Keoghan," Erica smiled. "We're so happy you're here for another year."

"Let's keep it that way. Our girl can't give up on us yet," Siobhan added.

Keoghan laughed and exhaled. "I'm not giving up anytime soon."

"That's what I like to hear. Alright, let's try this cake."

The cake was enjoyed, and bets were made on if there would be any left. There was not.

"Okay," Celena grinned. "I know it's Kay's birthday, and we're supposed to be doing what she wants, but I want her to do one thing for us."

"Depending on what it is, I might say yes," Keoghan responded.

"I want you... to try drag," Celena told her.

Keoghan's eyes widened. "Me? Be a drag king? In front of you?"

"Or queen," Chloe told her. "I think it's a great idea."

"Do it, do it, do it!" Siobhan chanted. "Damn, I would have brought my makeup if I knew we'd be getting a drag persona here."

Keoghan smiled. "Alright. I'll do it."

Thirty minutes later, Keoghan came out of her room wearing Celena's old suit that she had borrowed all those months ago for Halloween. Her face was contoured to look more masculine, and she had used mascara to create a fake mustache following a video tutorial. She wore glistening blue eyeshadow and what the online world called 'guyliner', and her hair was combed messily.

"Do you like it?" she asked timidly as she walked into the living room.

"Holy shit," Siobhan smiled. "You look amazing."

Erica nodded. "It doesn't look like it's your first try."

"It's..." Keoghan's voice trailed off. "It's not."

It was two in the morning, and Keoghan padded into her bathroom. She had been waking up in the early hours of the morning, unable to fall back asleep. Many times, she remembered the feeling of freedom when she saw the drag artists at Pride. After the first few sleepless nights, she had taken to staring at her makeup in the bathroom. It didn't take long until she plugged her earbuds into her phone, began watching drag tutorials, and recreated them on herself.

"Keoghan Winchester, amateur drag king," Celena smiled. "Have a name yet?"

"Not yet."

Elizabeth giggled softly. "Chris Kay."

"I like it. What made you think of that?" Keoghan asked.

"Well, you look like a Chris. And you're Kay!"

"Chris Kay. Well, I guess it's Chris Kay's birthday, too," Keoghan smiled.

"Happy birthday, Chris Kay!" Siobhan laughed. "A toast!"

"To Chris Kay!" the group chorused.

"To Chris Kay," Keoghan murmured. "Happy birthday."

They held up their wine glasses, and Keoghan smiled. She was being herself, and her friends loved her for it. She didn't need to hide anymore. Not with the people she was with.

"Okay, now give us a show!" Siobhan told her. "Celena, play music!"

Celena nodded, an evil grin growing on her face. "I know exactly what to play."

Rock music began to fill the room, and Keoghan recognized the song as one Celena played often.

"Of course you'd pick MSI," she laughed. "Alright. Let's do this."

"Fucking with me now, and it's all that I have and you're all that I want..."

Her confidence began to grow as she placed one foot on the coffee table and ran her hand up her leg. She leaned forward as she did, moving fluidly.

"Because seven minutes in heaven is all that I need when I get with him, seven minutes in heaven, I hope in the end that I'm not a virgin..."

Snapping back up, she strutted down the "catwalk" between the furniture in the center of the room and the sideboard against the wall.

"Hell yeah, Chris Kay!" Celena whooped.

She smiled widely and flashed them a wink. Something about performing, embodying Chris Kay, even if it was just for her friends, made her feel alive. She was truly Keoghan Winchester, Chris Kay, whoever she wanted to be. All it took was the right people.

Celena stopped the song, and applause sounded from around the room.

"Loved it," Celena smiled.

Iris stood up and took Keoghan's hand. "If you told yourself from a year ago that you'd be performing as a drag king for your girlfriend and friends, some of whom you met in rehab... Do you think she'd believe you?"

"Absolutely not," Keoghan laughed. "But that's the beauty of it."

"Fuck yeah," Siobhan agreed. "Keep it going, Chris Kay. Keep it going."

After everyone left, Keoghan, Iris, and Celena ran the dishwasher and cleaned up. Keoghan removed her Chris Kay makeup, though she kept the suit on. Celena went to bed, leaving Keoghan and Iris in the living room.

"I wish we could have gone to high school together," Iris sighed as they sat on the couch, music playing softly in the background. "Gone to Prom."

"Yeah," Keoghan nodded. "I went to mine with a son of my parents' friends."

"I went to mine alone."

"Watchin' every motion in my foolish lover's game, on this endless ocean, finally lovers know no shame..."

An idea struck Keoghan, and she stood up. "Dance with me."

Iris smiled and took her hand. "I would be honored."

"Watchin' in slow motion as you turn around and say: take my breath away..."

Keoghan placed her hand on Iris's waist and swayed to the music with her. Iris leaned her head against Keoghan's neck and kissed it.

"I'm so happy to be here with you," she murmured. "I love you."

"I love you too," Keoghan responded breathily.

"Through the hourglass I saw you, in time you slipped away. When the mirror crashed, I called you and turned to hear you say: 'If only for today, I am unafraid.' Take my breath away..."

Every inch of Keoghan's body was calm, yet electric. She held Iris close and ran her fingers through her hair.

"You're beautiful. And I'm so proud of you for coming out today."

Iris pressed her forehead against Keoghan's and smiled.

"I wouldn't have done it if you hadn't been there. So, thank you. Thank you for existing and loving me."

"I will love you until my heart is ripped out of my chest. Is it safe with you?"

"Forever."

"My love, take my breath away..."

38

Soledad smiled at Keoghan as they sat in her office. "How have you been this week?"

Keoghan nodded slowly. "Surreal. It's like... nothing's going wrong anymore. I have my life together."

"That's great to hear! I'm glad you're getting some reprive from the down side of life."

"Yeah," Keoghan exhaled. "It doesn't feel right, though."

"In what way?" Soledad asked.

"It's not how it should be, or at least I feel like it. I'm so used to pain and bad things that I can't believe my life will ever be good long-term."

"I see. That's a difficult belief to challenge."

"I don't know if I want to challenge it. At least this way I'll be prepared for whatever happens."

"Do you want to live in constant preparation for pain, though?"

"Not really, but maybe it's better that way," Keoghan sighed.

Soledad shook her head. "It isn't. You need to learn to live again."

"Live. Right."

"I know it's hard, but I have faith in you. Let's talk about some ways you can try to start..."

Keoghan listened, but she didn't truly comprehend anything Soledad was saying. Everything felt too fresh.

Still. Living.

Maybe she could try to live.

Siobhan and Erica invited Keoghan and Iris over to their apartment for a housewarming party a few days later. As the two women waited at the door, Keoghan looked around. There was a flowerpot with a small pride flag in it, and a windchime with wooden, colorful fish hanging next to the door.

"It's our girls!"

Keoghan smiled as Siobhan opened the door. "Hey, Siobhan."

"They're here? Oh, I'm not ready," Erica cried. "Come in, come in. I guess I'll have to postpone my grand makeup plans."

"Can we get a tour?" Keoghan asked, stepping inside. Iris followed her.

"Nice necklace," Iris told Siobhan. Keoghan looked at the woman's collarbone area- she was, in fact, wearing a necklace. It was a simple chain with a guitar pick hanging from it.

"Chay made it for me," Siobhan smiled, rubbing her finger against it. "We went to a basement show the day after your party, and I caught a guitar pick. She turned it into a necklace."

Iris nodded. "Sweet. We need to check out the show scene around our place, Keoghan."

"That'd be awesome," Keoghan affirmed.

Siobhan led them through the house, starting in a kitchen similar to Keoghan's. The living room was cozy, with assorted beanbags around a tiny table. Keoghan recognized some furniture from Finch's house.

"Our room," Siobhan announced, flinging open a door.

"You guys share a room?" Iris asked.

Erica nodded. "We, uh..."

"That's my girlfriend, suckers!" Siobhan laughed. "Rehab girls for the win."

Keoghan laughed along. "I never would have thought to go to rehab for a date."

"Neither did I," Erica said. "But I met Sio, and... yeah."

"I'm happy for you," Keoghan told them. "We all need someone to love."

"Chay makes the world a bit less shitty," Siobhan smiled.

Iris nodded and took Keoghan's hand. "I get that feeling about Keoghan."

"Why do you call her Chay?" Keoghan asked. "I need to get nick-name-ing tips for Iris."

"It's the last two letters of her name. Ca. Just... fancy," Siobhan explained. "Sorry. That's not a good tip."

"It's cute," Keoghan responded. "I'll figure something out."

A timer went off, and Erica hurried to the kitchen. "My chicken bake is ready!"

Everyone followed her out of the bedroom.

"Sit around the living room table," Siobhan instructed. "We haven't found an actual eating table yet. I'm going to go grab a hot pad."

Disappearing into the kitchen, Siobhan left Iris and Keoghan alone. Iris laid her head on Keoghan's shoulder and smiled.

"I'm so glad you met Siobhan and Erica," she murmured. "I think they're going to be your friends for a long time."

Keoghan nodded. "I think they will. We're going to be good for each other."

After they ate, Siobhan smiled and pointed to her guitar, which was leaning against the couch. "I think we should get the old girl out."

Iris nodded. "I forgot you played guitar."

"I want to hear you play again," Keoghan told her. "And Erica's singing."

"If you insist," Erica laughed.

Siobhan stood up and got the instrument, sitting back down on the large arm of the couch. "Let's rock this shit."

She unhooked her necklace and slid the pick off of it, then began to play.

"Chay's favorite song," she said softly to nobody in particular.

Erica placed one hand on Siobhan's knee and closed her eyes.

"Burning on, just like the match you strike to incinerate the lives of every-one you know..."

Iris nodded along, leaning on Keoghan's shoulder. "MCR. Sweet."

"I need to get more into their music," Keoghan laughed.

"Yeah, you do," Iris responded, joining Erica in singing.

"What's the worst that I can say? Things are better if I stay..."

"So long and goodnight," Siobhan trilled.

Erica kissed her knee and leaned against it. *"So long and goodnight."*

Keoghan wrapped her arm around Iris's waist. She waited until the chorus came around again and kissed Iris's cheek.

"So long and goodnight."

"Never so long, never goodnight," Iris murmured.

Siobhan leaned down to kiss the top of Erica's head, her eyes distant. *"So long and goodnight."*

That night, Keoghan and Iris watched a movie on Keoghan's laptop. Celena was out, though Keoghan didn't know where.

The movie was interesting, a silent film about power dynamics and the flaws of society called Metropolis. Iris's friend from high school had recommended it, but she had never gotten around to watching it. Keoghan was happy to see it with her. After it ended, Iris retired to their room.

Keoghan was washing dishes when she got the call.

"Celena Asher passed away in a car accident."

39

KEOGHAN'S SECOND INTERLUDE

There was something about losing Celena that was different from Lukas and Eri, losing Finch.

Keoghan shattered.

She came to in a graveyard. Her head spun, her muscles ached, and she knew there was only one thing that would make it better. She looked at the tombstone in front of her.

Finch's tombstone.

On it lay a single syringe and needle, next to a glass scale. Keoghan picked up the syringe and inspected it.

"Put it down," a familiar voice said.

No.

No.

She turned around. Lukas stood behind her, his rope bruises and cuts clearly visible, his cropped shirt showing more on his stomach and sides that Keoghan never knew about.

"What are you doing here?" Keoghan asked. "Are... are you a ghost? Why am I in a graveyard?"

"I'm coming to help you. I met Celena and Eri. They're coming as well," he said.

"What do you mean?"

Lukas sat down next to Keoghan. *"This is a dream. We can't come back in real life, but we can in your head. We're keeping William away, too."*

"Kay..."

Keoghan looked up. Celena stood over her, bloodied and bruised.

"I'm so fucking sorry, Kay," Celena cried. *"I... I shouldn't have gone out."*

"Don't blame yourself," Keoghan whispered, standing up to wrap the girl in her arms. "You didn't do anything wrong. I promise you, nobody thinks you're at fault."

A tap on her shoulder. Eri stood behind her and smiled, their face ashen.

"Hey, roommate."

Tears pricking at her eyes, Keoghan opened her arms for Eri to join the hug.

"Lukas, you too," she whispered.

Keoghan closed her eyes as she was held by the three, sobs racking her body.

What had she done to deserve this?

40

CELENA'S INTERLUDE

"Used to be one of the rotten ones and I liked you for that..."
Celena Asher sat in her room, listening to music and blowing smoke out of a vape. It was cherry flavored, bought because she hat hit her best friend's cherry vape and liked it. She loved the feeling nicotine gave her, the sleepy, happy feeling.

The door flung open, and she shoved it in her pocket.
"Celena. Celena, Celena, Celena."

Celena sometimes wished her name wasn't so easy to roll off the tongue. She wished she wasn't so "easy". She wished pleasing others *was* easy. She wished...

"Ce-le-na."

"What?" she groaned, turning around. "I'm busy."

"Busily being not busy, I'd say," her older brother, Wes, chuckled. "Seriously, though, I'm here to remind you that Mom wants you on the pitch in five minutes."

Raking a hand through her hair, Celena stood up and grabbed her soccer bag. "Alright. Let's go."

Wes left the room, and she took one last hit before shoving her vape in her desk drawer. He led her downstairs and opened the passenger door of his car for her. "You know, you don't have to try for Stanford. There are other schools that you can go to."

"No," Celena said firmly. "I'm going to Stanford, even if I have to kill for it."

"I don't think you'll have to do that," Wes laughed.

"You never know."

When they arrived at the soccer pitch- only a few minutes away from their house- Celena shouldered her bag and exited the car. Her mother stood on the green with her hands on her hips.

"You're late."

"By thirty seconds. Let's get started."

Celena gave her all, just as she did every time.
Stanford welcomed her with open arms.
"Park that car, drop that phone, sleep on the floor, dream about me..."
Celena welcomed death just as openly.

ACT SEVEN: ROT

41

Chloe and Elizabeth contacted the university and moved out of the dorms for the next semester, moving in with Keoghan and Iris. For the time being, Chloe would sleep on the couch and Elizabeth in Celena's old room.

Keoghan was a shell of herself. She lost weight again, refusing to eat anything other than strawberries. She didn't go out. There wasn't anything that she liked anymore.

At Iris's insistence, she scheduled an emergency session with Soledad, but it didn't help. She tried every coping skill she had learned at the clinic, but they didn't help. Nothing was working.

One day, she received a text from Erica.

Keoghan

I need you right now

Call me.

She immediately dialed Erica's number.

"What happened?" she asked.

"Siobhan..." Erica sobbed. "She's missing."

42

SIOBHAN'S INTERLUDE

Siobhan Clair had been many things. She had been a rockstar, an addict, a sister, a girlfriend. Now, she wanted to be dead.

She tried so hard. She tried so hard to be clean, sober, to recover, but it never stuck. So she found herself on the streets once again, smoking weed in a dingy bar while she waited for Aster, her plug.

"If it isn't Miss Rehab," Aster chuckled, placing a hand on her shoulder. "Back so soon?"

"Cut the shit and give me the stuff."

"Alright, but I'll warn you, it's strong this time."

"Good."

Half-Moon Bay resident Siobhan Clair found dead after injecting fentanyl-laced heroin. She will be missed by her girlfriend and friends. Clair's funeral will be held at...

43

SIOBHAN'S PRELUDE

"One, two, one, two, three, four!"

Siobhan began to strum her electric guitar and stepped up to the microphone, waiting for her cue. Her drummer, Maddi, set the rhythm as her bassist, Lex, plucked at her strings. Finally, the keyboardist Avery joined in.

"*Black sheep, come home, black sheep, come home, black sheep, come home…*"

Sending a glance back to Lex, Siobhan began to play more intensely.

"*Hello again, friend of a friend, I knew you when our common goal was waiting for the world to end…*"

Lex walked forward and stopped behind Siobhan.

"Come with me tonight," she murmured.

Siobhan nodded and slid her fingers across her guitar strings, sending Lex a wink. "Always."

Avery leaned close to the microphone attached to her keyboard and began to sing the verses that Siobhan knew so well, leaving her to focus on the riffs. Siobhan had asked for a Type O Negative-style guitar solo, which Avery had honored almost too well: the solo sounded almost exactly like that in *I Don't Wanna Be Me*. Even though the song was a cover, they had made it truly their own: a metal take on Metric's classic *Black Sheep*.

Once the gig ended, the band packed their things and loaded them into Maddi's truck.

"Who am I driving home tonight?" Maddi asked, placing a hand on her hip. She was tall, with cropped bubblegum-pink hair and large black colored contacts. Her homemade black band tee shouted "Constella Will Eat Your Children", an inside joke in their band, Constella. A studded belt held up her black cargo pants, and she had made her own studded Docs.

Avery raised her small hand. She was Maddi's polar opposite- four foot, eleven inches tall despite being a Junior in high school, long black hair up in twin ponytails, and purple glasses. Her pink band tee was marked with all four girls' handprints and the Constella logo on the back.

"I'm going home with Lex," Siobhan told the others, running a hand over her buzzed hair. She had cut it off a few days prior on a whim. Well, a high whim- but a whim all the same. She didn't regret it yet.

Maddi shook her head, though it was clear there was love behind it as she smiled. "Alright. Here, I made you your shirt."

She handed Siobhan a black t-shirt with "Constella Will Make You Come (back for more)" bleached into the back and handprints on the chest.

"Hell yeah," Siobhan smiled. "I love it."

Lex stepped down from the truck bed and wrapped her arms around Siobhan's waist. Siobhan inspected her new nails- purple claws with short nails on her playing hand. They matched her purple bob and band shirt ("Constella Take The World").

"You gonna put those short nails to good use?" Avery laughed.

"Yeah, like this," Lex responded, giving her the finger. "What I do with Siobhan isn't any of your business. Unless you wanna join."

"And hook up with you? No way."

"Ladies, ladies... settle down," Siobhan smirked. "Aves, Mad, I'll see you tomorrow for practice."

"Bye, Siobhan! Don't get an STD," Maddie responded. "And bye, Lex. Don't give Siobhan an STD."

"I don't have any STDs," Lex argued. "I got tested, like, a week ago."

"Whatever you say. Come on, Aves, I have a curfew."

Maddi and Avery got into the truck and backed away, leaving Siobhan with Lex.

"Come on, baby," Lex murmured, spinning Siobhan around to face her. "Let's get out of here."

"Hell yeah," Siobhan smiled. "Let's go."

44

SIOBHAN'S LOVE

Siobhan came to in Lex's bed. The smell of marijuana floated through the room, and she felt Lex's skin against hers.

"Hey, baby," Lex whispered, exhaling smoke. "Welcome to the world of the living."

"Hey, yourself. Gimme," Siobhan smiled, reaching for Lex's blunt and taking a long hit.

Lex brushed a strand of hair out of Siobhan's face and trailed her fingers down her neck and along her collarbone. "Someday, you gotta start buying your own."

"Someday, I will." Siobhan reached for her phone to check the time. "Shit. It's already 11."

"What, like you're actually going to go to class?"

"Fair point."

Siobhan grabbed her bra and put her arms through it. Like she always did, Lex hooked it, allowing her fingers to caress Siobhan's back.

"Can I borrow one of your shirts?" Siobhan asked.

Lex laughed. "If you bring it back this time. Here, you want my Sisters of Mercy shirt?"

"Hell yeah."

Slipping it on, Siobhan smiled. Lex's shirts were always baggy and long, something that she could never find in shirts she bought.

Lex put on her own clothes and walked over to Siobhan, looping her finger through her jeans.

"Are we going anywhere?"

Siobhan traced her finger along Lex's jawline. "Not unless you want to."

"Downstairs might be nice," Lex murmured, leaning in to kiss her. "But there's no rush."

"Let's go. You know I can't do shit until I'm caffeinated."

With coffee in hand, the two girls decided to take Lex's car on a drive along the beach. They lived in Los Angeles, so it wasn't too far of a drive to get there. As they sped along the road, Siobhan suddenly noticed a car coming at them in the same lane.

"Shit, Lex, watch out-"

Breaks screeching. Pain. Glass. A deployed airbag.

The world went black.

45

LEX'S INTERLUDE

Siobhan was given every shirt that Lex owned.

Other than that, she didn't remember much of what happened after.

Lex was replaced with a girl Siobhan didn't know.

Siobhan shot up with her. Her thoughts became more fragmented. She moved in with her. The band fell apart. Maddi moved away, Avery was murdered in a parking lot shooting.

When the girl died, Siobhan couldn't even remember her name.

46

SIOBHAN'S FIRST STAY

"Another?" Siobhan groaned, sitting up and inspecting her hand. There was a small tattoo of a cross on her middle finger. She looked around, discovering that she lay on a couch in what appeared to be a basement.

Standing, she pulled on the shirt she had brought with her- Lex's Limp Bizkit shirt- and walked up the stairs. She came out into an apartment complex and sighed. Fuck.

Her phone rang. When she looked at the Caller ID, she saw that it was her sister.

"Siobhan, get your ass into rehab," her sister said as soon as she took a look at her through the phone. "I swear to God, if you don't go, I'm going to block you. On everything."

"I'm fine, Isha," Siobhan responded. "I swear. Besides, I... I don't have the money."

"We'll see about putting it on my insurance. I will fly out tonight and drive you if I have to."

"Are you serious about blocking me?" Siobhan whispered. "You know I can't take that."

Isha sighed and nodded. "You need to get help. I promise, it'll be worth it. Just try."

And so, Siobhan found herself in a rehab center in Sunnyvale for the first time. It was in Northern California, but her escapades had taken her close enough to make it the best option. She kept all her things in a duffle bag which she brought with her, and as soon as she arrived she took inventory of her shirts. One caught her eye, and she pulled it out of the pile.

"Constella Will Make You Come (back for more)," she murmured, memories flooding through her. "Constella..."

Without a second thought, she pulled it on.

A woman walked into the room with a smile. "Siobhan? Dinner's ready."

Siobhan nodded and followed her out of the room. She joined a few other women in the kitchen, where they were serving quinoa salad.

"Is that a band?" one woman asked, pointing at Siobhan's shirt. "Dig the tit-handprints."

"Yeah," Siobhan replied. "My band. And thanks. The drummer made it."

"Every artist is a junkie," another laughed. "Welcome to the family."

When Siobhan was discharged, nobody said goodbye.

Some family she had found.

47

ISHA'S INTERLUDE

Siobhan called Isha every Sunday, sometimes other times throughout the week. One Sunday, Isha didn't pick up no matter how many times Siobhan called.

Strange. Siobhan assumed she was sleeping; she had just been through a bad breakup and had no energy left after dealing with her fucked-up ex. She scrolled through her phone's newsfeed, and saw an article from Isha's hometown. After reading it, she checked out the rest of the town's digital newspaper. One article caught her eye.

"Isha?" she whispered, seeing her sister's name in the headline.

Isha Clair murdered by ex-boyfriend, no next of kin.

Siobhan read it again.

Isha Clair murdered by ex-boyfriend, no next of kin.
Isha Clair
Murdered
By Ex-Boyfriend
No next of kin.

Siobhan set down her phone and stared at the wall.

"Isha..."

Siobhan Clair, back to junkie life.

Siobhan Clair sent to rehab again, barely any money for bills.

Siobhan Clair meets girl, falls in love, finds it too good to be true.

Siobhan Clair destroys everything she touches.

Siobhan Clair.

What good was there in being Siobhan Clair? Dead parents. Dead sister. Dead friends. Dead everyone. Dead. Dead, dead, dead.

Was there anything that wouldn't die? She couldn't even keep a flower alive. She couldn't keep anyone's trust in her alive- except Isha and Erica. Maybe Keoghan. And then, she couldn't keep Isha alive. She wouldn't be able to keep Erica alive. Lord knew how much longer Keoghan would be alive.

Dead. Everyone was dead.

Siobhan Clair,

Finally dead as well.

48

SIOBHAN'S POSTLUDE

Siobhan opened her eyes. She lay on a couch in a brick room. A familiar song was pulsing through the walls.

"Black sheep, come home, black sheep, come home, black sheep, come home..."

"What the fuck?" she murmured.

Standing, she looked around. She seemed to be in a basement, and there were stairs leading up to what she hoped was the ground floor. Climbing them, she took note of the house's layout and design. There were band posters everywhere, and one caught her eye.

Constella. It was the poster she and her friends had only made four copies of, one for each band member. Her poster had gone missing in her trek across California.

"What the fuck?" she asked again. "Hello?"

She continued to walk through the house until she found a door and exited. She stepped out into a wheat field, where a single speaker stood in front of her. On it sat a blue-and-pink-haired woman, smiling and singing the lyrics to the song that was pulsing through Siobhan's veins.

"I'll send you my love on a wire, lift you up every time everyone pulls away from you..."

"Hey, Sio. You finally made it," the woman smiled, music fading as she stopped singing.

Siobhan nodded slowly. "Where exactly have I made it?"

"To forever."

49

Keoghan was barely holding on, sinking her claws into whatever she could to prevent a further spiral. Celena was gone. Siobhan was gone. Lukas, Eri, everyone was gone.

"I'm cursed," Keoghan told Soledad in their second emergency session of the month. "That's the only way to explain it. I'm the constant in all of their lives."

"You aren't cursed, Keoghan. I validate your pain and your need for an explanation, but you aren't cursed," Soledad responded.

"I feel cursed. I feel like... I feel like the only way to save my friends is to die," Keoghan sobbed. "I don't know what to do."

"Death wouldn't save anyone. In fact, it could lead to suicide from your loved ones should their grief go untreated. You deserve to live."

"I know that in theory, I just..."

"It's hard. But you will survive. Your homework this week is to survive."

After Keoghan went home, she fell asleep. When she opened her eyes, there was only darkness. Darkness and cold. She looked to the right, nothing. To the left stood a brown chair with a bloodred cushion.

"It's like my old hair," she whispered, laughing nervously. "What the fuck is going on?"

She looked around again. No one, nothing, just a cold void and a chair. Carefully, she walked to the chair and ran her hands over the armrests. A jacket was draped over the back- had it always been there? Keoghan picked it up and inspected it. It was a black leather jacket with brown patches over the sleeves, something she swore she saw Eri wear once. She cast one more glance around the void and put it on. Instantly, she felt protected. The cold receded, and a pinprick of light was visible in the distance. Something told her to walk to it, so she did.

As she walked, she saw the splotch of light grow larger and take on a form. It seemed like it was moving toward her, and she swore she could hear the sound of a voice coming from it.

"Keo, Keo..."

Her eyes widened, and she shook her head. "No."

"Keo, look! I won my class's mock election!"

There was only one person who ever called her Keo.

Lukas.

Tears began to prick at her eyes, and she broke into a run toward the light.

"Do you think I'll make it onto the Student Council in high school? Maybe even the President!"

She remembered his first Student Council election vividly. He won by a landslide.

"You know, when you're in high school, you'll be able to find a boyfriend! Maybe if you really love him, your parents won't make you marry some random guy. If I could, I'd marry you."

"That's incest, Reg."

The wall she put up to barricade her tears cracked and burst as she heard her own voice being played back to her, talking to him. She would never get to do that again. Why was she here? What had she done to deserve this, the torture of hearing her interactions with the boy she loved more than anyone else? Was it to rub salt in the wound that just as she had figured out how she could relate to him, empathize with him, he was taken from her?

"I think you'll find a nice guy. Or, you know, maybe a girl."

"I'm not gay."

"Would it be that bad if you were?"

"No," Keoghan sobbed, raising a hand to touch the light. "Reg, I have to tell you. I'm bisexual. I found a girl. It's not bad that I'm gay, or, well, somewhat gay. Queer. It's not bad at all."

Sobs began to rack her body, and she folded in on herself, hugging her arms to her chest. The light convulsed, twisting in on itself in a grotesque manner. Keoghan looked away. She didn't want to see the light that had been Lukas move in such an unnatural way.

When the light worked itself out, it was a slightly different person-shape.

"Hey! I'm Eri. Are you my roommate?"

"Eri?" Keoghan whispered, voice breaking. "I'm so sorry. Eri, I miss you like family."

Choking out a cry, Keoghan knelt on the floor as the light changed shape again.

"You know, Kay, I'm saving the kids. All the kids. I'm such a great role model."

"Celena..."

"You gotta keep that fire burning. Don't let anyone piss on it or throw it into the water."

Keoghan nodded. "I know. I know, Siobhan. I'm trying to keep my fire alive."

The light began to spark and catch flame, the roaring heat blanketing Keoghan's body. She took off the jacket and, inspecting it one more time, threw it into the fire. It swallowed the offering and molded itself into a single bead of radiating glow, a distant yet close voice radiating from it. Lukas was speaking again.

"Hey, Keo. I just wanted to say that I'm sorry for not telling you how I was feeling. I couldn't hide myself anymore, and I kept it all inside even though I told you to do the opposite. I can't say I wouldn't do it again, but I regret it. I regret keeping you in the dark until that dark swallowed me. I think we could have changed the world together. You still can. Keoghan, live with love and fire. I met Siobhan, and she told me about your inextinguishable flame. You have to keep it going, Keo. I love you forever."

Keoghan reached for the light, but it flickered and darted away from her grasp.

"I have to go. I want you to stay alive, but when the time comes... don't be afraid. You'll see me again. Goodnight, Keo. Reg and the Jester forever."

The light extinguished itself, and Keoghan was left alone in the dark.

"Keep that fire burning," she heard a voice echo. *"And pour out a drink for me. Red wine or whiskey."*

Keoghan nodded, laughing gently. "I will, Siobhan."

"You'd better."

"Keep on trucking, Keoghan," Eri's voice told her.

"I'll truck 'till I run out of gas."

Another voice began to fill the void. *"I love you, Kay. I'll be waiting for you."*

Waiting for you, waiting for you, waiting for you, echoed throughout the space. *I'll be waiting for you.*

Keoghan closed her eyes again. "I'll see you again, Celena."

Then, she woke up.

Iris lay peacefully next to her, soft exhales inside while the road droned outside. Keoghan brushed stray hair out of Iris's face and lightly kissed her cheek.

It was time to sleep dreamlessly.

The next day, Keoghan was hit by the reality of death again. William had been gone for a long time, but there was still a voice in her head telling her that everything that happened was her fault and hers alone. Her fault for living, for being in the lives of those who passed. Everyone close to her would die, and she would be to blame.

"Hey," Iris's voice said from afar. "Keoghan."

Keoghan blinked. She was laying on the couch, using Iris as a head-rest.

"Are you okay?" Iris asked.

"I need to break up with you," Keoghan murmured.

Iris looked taken aback. "Why is that?"

"Because," Keoghan sniffed, "if I don't, you're going to die."

"I'm not going to die, Keoghan. I promise you, I'm going to stay alive."

"You can't promise that. You're not immortal."

"Pretend I am. Pretend I'm immortal, pretend I'm a spirit haunting you, whatever you need. You aren't breaking up with me because of death," Iris insisted. "If we don't live now, if you hide from me because you're worried I'll die, you're sentencing yourself to spiritual death. Would you tell Erica not to be with Siobhan because she died?"

Keoghan shook her head, tears beginning to bead in her eyes. "No."

"Then stay. Please. Stay with me," Iris begged, leaning down to kiss Keoghan's forehead.

Closing her eyes, Keoghan melted into her. "My immortal girl-friend..."

"Your immortal Iris."

50

THE SONG

As Erica and Keoghan worked on sorting through Siobhan's things, something neither of them could fully wrap their minds around doing, they came across a small green notebook tucked behind Siobhan's guitar.

"What should we do with this?" Keoghan asked, holding it up.

Erica, emotionless, shrugged. "I don't want to read it. We can burn it."

"Alright..." Keoghan said warily. She was worried about Erica. The woman hadn't been eating, she hadn't been going out...

As she placed the notebook on the table, a piece of paper fluttered out. Keoghan picked it up.

"To Erica," she read aloud. "In case I don't make it..."

Erica's eyes widened, and her numbness seemed to crack. "What? Read more."

"In case I don't make it, I have something for you. I don't have any recordings, just the lyrics. I love you."

Keoghan handed the paper to Erica, whose eyes began to brim with tears.

"*I'm staring at my bedroom walls,*" Erica sang softly. "*Wondering when they'll belong to a hospital. I'm staring at your photo frame, thinking 'bout how I couldn't say your name.*"

Her voice cracked, and she wiped her eyes.

"I love you, baby, come back down from Heaven. I love you baby. Do you regret what you did?"

Erica began to sob the words, and Keoghan worried she would choke.

"Oh, I love you, baby. When I found out what happened, I cried until I followed you."

Taking a deep breath in, Erica smiled through her tears.

"I know that's what you'll have to say, I'm sorry that I went away, but I love you, baby, so try your best to stay."

51

Keoghan returned to Stanford for her fall semester. She worked at the coffee shop. She hung out with her friends. Chris Kay made appearances in the school's queer social scene. She attempted to recover from her eating disorder for good. Life was normal. She was normal. Everything was normal.

But it wasn't.

In their second year, Chloe committed suicide- or, at least, Keoghan thought she did. Chloe had been found dead in a car crash, where her and Elizabeth's vehicle was wrapped around the only stop sign for miles in a field. Elizabeth wasn't with her at the time. There was no way that was an accident, Chloe had been the best driver out of the group. Soledad attempted to point out that she could have been under the influence, but Keoghan fought back. It was better for her and her friends to think Chloe's death was a suicide. The idea that Chloe, who had finally seemed to enjoy life, had it robbed from her... Keoghan didn't want to think about it.

Erica was sent back to rehab. Without Siobhan to hold her, with Keoghan always at school, she had slipped through the cracks. Keoghan called her as often as she could, but it was clear that her fire had been stomped out for good. She never laughed, never smiled, and her eyes were hollow.

Erica had given up.

Despite her efforts not to give in, Keoghan's skin became littered with more little red lines. She fell back onto her eating disorder. Iris tried her best to pull her out of the hole she was digging, and even when it seemed like Keoghan would never see the sun, Iris held on.

Her parents cut off all contact with her. Keoghan often wondered why she wasn't more hurt by it. Maybe it was because she had seen it coming. After the drugs, after the rehab costs... she wished them well and moved on.

Iris stayed by her side through everything. Iris, Immortal Iris. Keoghan loved her until she couldn't think straight, loved her until she was sure she could never love another again.

Erica left rehab, but she was never the same. One day, she disappeared and stopped answering her phone. Keoghan didn't believe in any God, but she prayed to whatever was out there that Erica would come back.

She never did.

Keoghan, Iris, and Elizabeth graduated. Life moved on. Elizabeth became an English teacher at a local high school. Iris took over her family company with Keoghan at her side. They lived happily, or as happy as they could be. Keoghan began to meet with a dietician.

Still, every day, every time Keoghan had a second to think, she remembered her losses. Lukas, Eri, Celena, Finch, Siobhan, Chloe,. All the death, all the people taken too soon, Erica, who was still missing. She talked to Soledad, but it seemed like a formality. Everyone who saw her knew she was barely holding on.

She moved to Portland with Iris after half a year. Elizabeth called, but they were never as close as they had been before.

She remembered William and Balthy. They never bothered her again, but she felt them in her mind, watching her. Whenever she saw a man with that angular face that William had, Balthy's strange build, she felt her blood run cold. Iris held her hand tighter, and she sped away as fast as she could.

She kept a candle burning for Lukas on her dresser, next to a framed picture of him. Sometimes, when she couldn't sleep, she'd look over at him and wish him well. Wish for him to keep the voices and thoughts away.

It wasn't all bad, though. She and Iris adopted a cat named Winston. The company did incredibly well under their management. Iris's parents invited them over for every holiday, Chinese and American. She began to claw her way out of her grave, holding onto every inch of sunlight that she could feel on her cold skin.

She was always grateful that despite everything, Iris was with her.

Iris would always be with her.

52

Chloe's Interlude

Chloe Maxwell's first thought of suicide came when she was nine. She remembered it vividly; it gave her comfort. Comfort to know that none of her friends could do anything because the issue's roots had taken hold. Comfort to know that one day, she would make her nine-year-old self happy.

Her first partner had made a suicide pact with her. She was four years older than Chloe, but had insisted that they were soulmates. She sent her explicit texts despite Chloe's insistence not to. Eventually, Chloe gave in and played along. When the time to enact the pact came, her partner went through with it. Chloe did not.

In her Sophomore year of high school, she met Elizabeth Kelly. The two became inseparable, sharing every experience with each other and relating to the other's experiences with Borderline Personality Disorder and various eating disorders. Chloe had experience with anorexia since she could remember, and Elizabeth had ARFID.

"It's just like," Chloe began during a lunch period, "like... shit."

Elizabeth nodded sagely. "Shit is an appropriate word for this."

"They said our average lifespan is twenty-seven. That's such bullshit. You have to live longer than that, Liza."

"What about you, Chloe?" Elizabeth asked. "Are you going to live to twenty-seven?"

Chloe shrugged. "I guess we'll find out."

"How do you want to die?"

All of the other friends Chloe had showed distaste for her apathy toward her own life, but Elizabeth understood. Whenever Chloe spiraled, Elizabeth was there. Whenever Elizabeth did, Chloe was. They had a closer relationship than most friends, but neither saw the need to engage romantically- they were more like sisters.

"I want to die in a way that I control."

When they arrived at Stanford, they chose to room separately. Still, they kept in contact and hung out as much as they could.

The only thing Chloe regretted about her suicide was leaving Elizabeth behind and totalling their car. She took her prescribed sleep meds- more than she should, though she didn't bother counting pills- and climbed into the vehicle, head thundering yet swimming.

It was time to make everything go away.

53

ERICA'S INTERLUDE

Erica Junie was never meant to stay around for long. She was meant to live fast, die young, and love boldly. If she hadn't met Finch, if he hadn't gotten her on the drugs, maybe she could have loved boldly in a place that wasn't the afterlife. Maybe she wouldn't have gone to rehab twice and still ended up dead.

Maybe someone would have known that she died.

In her last moments, she felt someone slipping a leather jacket over her shoulders as she sat hunched in an alleyway. She knew nobody was there, but she swore she saw a flash of green and pink hair in her peripheral vision.

Siobhan. Loud, sweet, genuine Siobhan had taught her the true meaning of loving boldly. It wasn't about sex or drinking contests, yelling or drugs. It was about staying together even when every piece of the world was falling apart. Holding hands as the storm hit them face-on.

"Siobhan..." she whispered, cold wrapping her body as she struggled to lift her hand. "I love you."

She remembered a time when she and Siobhan had fought about if Siobhan was truly clean. Erica had been wondering what to do with the night, and Siobhan suggested getting a drink.

"We're not supposed to be doing that," Erica had said.

"Come on," Siobhan groaned. "We're not seriously gonna live like this forever?"

"There's more to life than drugs, Sio."

"The God of Wine comes, crashing through the headlights of a car that took you farther than you thought you'd ever want to go. We can't get back again..."

Siobhan scoffed. "I know that. I just want to have some fun."

"I don't think it's a good idea."

"I can't keep it all together, I know I can't keep it all together..."

"Then I'll go without you. I'm not doing drugs, Chay. I promise."

Erica sighed. "Please don't. I love you, Sio, and I don't want you getting hurt."

"And the God of Wine is crouched down in my room. You let me down, I said it, now I'm going down and you're not around..."

Darkness swallowed her, and her senses began to dim.

"...love you too," she heard in the distance. "I love you forever. And I'm sorry."

"And there's a memory of a window, looking through I see you searching for something I could never give you. And there's someone who understands you more than I do, a sadness I can't erase all alone on your face..."

Erica couldn't hear anything anymore.

She couldn't feel anything. It was like sleep when she was far too high, when dreams ceased and all that was left was a void of her own thoughts and feelings.

Then, she felt warmth.

She opened her eyes, and light flooded her vision. Long grass-wheat- tickled her skin. A song played from a large speaker in front of her. Music pulsed through her ears, though it wasn't the song she died mumbling.

"And when I'm begging for it to be over, I imagine you say: Can I stay for a little while? This isn't meaningless sex..."

"Hello?" she called.

A shadow stepped over her, and she turned around. A green-and-pink-haired woman stood over her with a smile. She wore a ratty t-shirt with handprints on the chest. The woman sat down next to her, and Erica read the back of the shirt.

"Constella Will Make You Come (back for more)," she laughed. "I love that."

"Aww, thank'ya, Chay."

Erica's eyes widened. "Siobhan?"

"In the flesh."

"Can I stay for a little while? This isn't meaningless sex, and I want to fall in love again..."

"Is this real?" Erica asked, holding her hands up to the sky. She felt Siobhan's warm palms touch her own, and the other woman nodded.

"It's forever. That's what your soul told me when I got here. Now come on, let's go inside."

"Do you love me despite my body? 'Cause I've seen the way you look at me, and you look at me like you're seeing me..."

Siobhan helped her up, and Erica followed her, not letting go of her hand.

"My... soul?" she asked as they strode through the seemingly endless field.

Nodding again, Siobhan stopped. "When I first arrived in this place, I saw you. The you thattold me that this place was where we would be until we were ready to move on, and that you would be here soon. Then, she left. I've been waiting for you."

"Can I stay for a little while? This isn't meaningless sex, and I want to fall in love again. Can you love me and all my body?"

Erica blinked, and a large traditionally German-style house appeared. The stonework on the bottom story was intricate, and the top portion had unique woodwork. Flowering ivy trellises covered the area beside the door, and large planter boxes were placed underneath the windows. They entered, and the music faded.

"What exactly is this? Is... is it Heaven?"

"I don't know. But I know that I get to share it with you, so it's heaven to me."

"Did you meet God?" Erica whispered.

"Chay, we both know that I gave up on that fantasy long ago. For all I know, this could be a trip. I don't care, though, and neither should you. If it's Heaven, great, if it's not... like I said, I don't care. You live and you die, Chay. Let's try to live on," Siobhan smiled. "For me?"

Erica nodded and returned the smile faintly. "Alright. We'll live on."

"That's my girl. Come on, let's go inside."

POSTLUDE: REGROWTH

It was a Monday, another Monday that would stretch on and tick away and eventually be left in the dust. Keoghan sat in her office at Iris's company and clicked through her e-mails. Suddenly, her phone rang. She kept it on silent mode, but Iris and Elizabeth were allowed to bypass it, even though she wasn't all too close with Elizabeth anymore.

To her surprise, Elizabeth was exactly who was calling.

"Hey, Liv," Keoghan greeted warmly. "It's been forever."

"It has. I'm sorry for not calling more, life's been hectic with teaching and... my girlfriend..." Elizabeth responded.

"Wait, Liv, you have a girlfriend?"

Elizabeth nodded. "Actually, that's why I'm calling. We're getting married, and I want you to be my maid of honor. I know it's a big ask, and we haven't talked in a while, but... as your 'boyfriend', it was only right."

Keoghan's face broke into a wide smile. She had forgotten that Elizabeth had been her 'boyfriend' during their college days. The memory was sweet and sour, bringing back times of joy yet reminders of Balthy and the things that had transpired during Keoghan's Freshman year.

Pushing those thoughts away, she nodded vigorously. Her friend was engaged and had thought of her. Keoghan nodded vigorously and pretended her thoughts hadn't wandered anywhere that wasn't Elizabeth's wedding.

"Oh my God, Liv, of course!" she cried. "I'm so happy for you. Tell me all about her. What's her name? Can I see a picture? Oh, this is so nice…"

"She's right here," Elizabeth laughed. "Hey, Angel, can you come here? My maid of honor wants to meet you."

A feminine giggle, and a second face appeared on the screen. She was tall, with tan skin and long charcoal hair accented by thick snow-colored stripes. Both of her eyebrows were pierced, one with two rings and the other with one, she had a chain on the bridge of her nose accented with a septum piercing, and a single ring on the left side of her lower lip.

"Hey, Keoghan," the woman smiled. "My name's Carmine. Liza's told me all about you."

Keoghan smiled back. "Nice to meet you, Carmine. I didn't know about you until now."

"Liza's been so busy, but we've been together since her Senior year at Stanford. That's… what… four years behind us."

"Jesus," Keoghan sighed. "Four years…"

"Are you and Iris…?" Elizabeth asked.

Keoghan shook her head. "Not yet. I've been wanting to propose, but I can't find the right time."

"And I thought we took the slow train. We'll help you," Elizabeth told her. "Have you been ring shopping at all?"

"Yeah. I actually have a ring, I just haven't gotten off my ass to do it yet."

Carmine took the phone from Elizabeth and nodded. "Alright. Here's what you're going to do…"

"You're going to take her to a nice place."

Keoghan and Iris went out to Iris's favorite restaurant, a hole-in-the-wall Italian restaurant. It wasn't exactly "nice", but it was Iris's favorite. Keoghan had learned to love it as she began to erode her walls around food, and eventually it became one of her favorites as well.

"You're going to bring her somewhere pretty. The ocean, maybe, or a botanic garden."

She drove her to Canon Beach at sunset, and they stood on a cliff facing the ocean for a long time, holding hands.

"And then... you're going to get out the ring and propose."

"Hey, Iris, look over there! The first star!" Keoghan cried, pointing behind Iris. There was no star, but she used the quick second to kneel down and pull out the box containing the ring. When Iris turned back around, she gasped.

"Iris, I love you," Keoghan told her, looking her in the eyes. "Will you marry me?"

Iris pulled Keoghan up and kissed her. "Oh my God. Yes."

Keoghan slipped the ring, an infinity symbol with a small sapphire in the center, onto Iris's hand.

"Actually..." Iris laughed, reaching into her purse. "I was going to do the same thing tonight."

Keoghan gasped as Iris took her turn to fall onto one knee and open a velvet box. "Keoghan... now that I've already given you my answer... will *you* marry me?"

Tears of joy began to cascade down Keoghan's cheeks. "Yes."

Elizabeth and Carmine's wedding took place a few weeks later in mid-June, held in a vineyard in California near their house. Golden and wine-red flowers decorated the venue, and Elizabeth wore a long white dress while Carmine's suit matched the maroon flowers. The summer air caressed Keoghan's skin, and she smiled widely the entire time.

There was nothing more beautiful than watching friends live their lives with love.

Keoghan remembered her dream about Lukas's wedding, but it didn't feel as sharp a sting. Her body didn't feel as alien, the dress didn't bring her as much panic, so she knew the world would be okay. Despite everything, the world would be okay.

Keoghan and Iris were married in October. Their friends (and Iris's family) celebrated with them until the early morning hours, after which the couple left for a short honeymoon in upstate New York to pay Keoghan's parents a visit. Keoghan hadn't spoken to them since she left rehab all those years ago, and she felt it was the right time to see them. As they drove, Iris looked over at her often with worry in her eyes. Keoghan tried to smile reassuringly, but she didn't know if it helped.

"Feel the rush of my blood, seventeen again... I am not scared of death, I've got dreams again..."

When the two women arrived at the Winchester house, Keoghan felt adrenaline pumping through her body. It was time.

"I don't even know if they live here anymore," she whispered. "Alright. Let's do this."

Iris gave her an encouraging smile. Keoghan rang the doorbell, and her mother opened the door.

"There is meaning on Earth, I am happy..."

"Keoghan?" she asked. "What are you doing here? You've gotten fat. What have you done to your hair? I'm not giving you any money, you know."

"I'm not coming here for money, Mother, nor do I need your comments on my appearance. I'm here to tell you that I've gotten married," Keoghan responded coolly.

"Where is your husband, then? Did he grow tired of you already?"

"I resent that. But no, there is no husband. This is my wife, Iris," Keoghan told her. "And I will not be taking any criticism of her. We have been together for more than seven years now, and I thought you should know."

"Of course you'd be a lesbian. You were always so ungrateful. Well, I will not stand for that. You are no longer welcome here, or anywhere near us or the Lancaster family. You may choose to live in sin, but you will do so alone."

Keoghan's mother turned on her heel and slammed the door closed.

"A minute from home and I feel so far from it..."

"I'm sorry, Keoghan," Iris murmured, pulling her into a hug. "Let's go."

Keoghan nodded and nestled her head into the crook of Iris's neck. "In a second. I need to say my goodbyes to this place. Make my peace."

"Of course," Iris smiled.

Breaking out of the hug, Keoghan kept Iris's hand in hers as she turned toward the door. She placed her free hand on the white wood and sighed deeply.

"None of you deserved me. None of you deserved Lukas. Not this house, not this money, not any of the things you got from the roulette of life. I'm sorry that I ever tried to fix things, because your fragile fucking ego can't take it. I'm sorry that you thought I'd come out of your mold as a perfect daughter and couldn't accept it when I had cracks," Keoghan told the door, her voice gaining strength as she spoke and her expression turning resolute. "But you know what? I'm not sorry that I have those cracks. Because I have Iris, I have my friends, I have a good life. I'm happy. I'm not a sinner. And if I go to Hell, I will see you there."

Turning away from the house, Keoghan led Iris to their rental car.

"You're free," Iris smiled, squeezing Keoghan's hand. "Does it hurt?"

Keoghan chuckled slowly. "Like a bitch. But you know what? It's fine. I don't need her. I don't need any of the people I was supposed to call my family. You, Liv, everyone I love has done more for me than they ever have and ever will."

"And we'll keep doing all that we can for you. Forever," Iris told her.

"Forever," Keoghan responded, kissing her cheek gently. "You broke my curse, Immortal Iris, so you'd better make good on that. I certainly plan to do it for you."

Iris laughed quietly, and the two women climbed into the car.

"Ready to go? For good?"

Keoghan gave one last glance to the building and nodded. "Let's leave this place in the dust."

They drove away from the Winchester house, the sunset in their rearview. Keoghan smiled as the building became nothing more than a speck behind them. She had Iris, and they were Mrs. and Mrs. Song. Everything would be okay. More than okay- life would be beautiful once again.

"The things that I lost here, the people I know, they got me surrounded for a mile or two. Left at the graveyard, I'm driving past ghosts. Their arms are extended, my eyes start to close. The car's in reverse, I'm gripping the wheel, I'm back between villages and everything's still."

AUTHOR'S NOTE

This book may seem like a series of traumatic events just for the sake of trauma, but it isn't. Every event in this book is inspired by events in my life, some of which are enhanced by my fears about how my own trauma could have been shaped.

This project started as a fanfiction that took me five years to complete, starting again from scratch halfway through. I wanted to tell a tragic story with a happy ending, and when the time came to turn it into an original novel I decided to do so by placing my life experiences onto Keoghan. It became especially important to me for her to have an eating disorder, as I have been struggling with my own for years. Her sexual trauma was even more important, with my own coming back to kick my ass over and over again. Loss. All the loss and the ugly, ugly spirals that come after. By the time I had listed out all the aspects of my being I wanted for her, I realized there were so many more that I could only gloss over. Self-harm addiction, for one. Borderline Personality Disorder as portrayed by Chloe and Elizabeth. This novel is nowhere near perfect, but I hope it can strike true with you the way every iteration of Keoghan's story has hit me.

For everyone out there struggling with any topics I mentioned in this novel, be it sexual abuse, drug abuse, self-harm, eating disorders, loss- there is hope. There is always hope, and whereas your feelings and thoughts may never go away to the extent that would be considered "normal", you can get out. You can survive. I wish you nothing but the best in your fight to live, and know that I am fighting alongside you. One day at a time, we will claw ourselves out of the graves we've dug and others have dug for us.

THANK YOU!

I cannot begin an acknowledgments section without thanking my number one hypewoman, best friend, and sister River. She's stuck with me throughout every single one of my writing phases, from my self-insert angel of darkness during the pandemic to my indulgent fanfiction. Kawa, you mean the world to me and it's a crime that we don't get to see each other more often. We'll live together one day, and you get to deal with me 24/7.

Next, of course, the rest of my family. Thank you all for supporting me from the days when I would steal your laptops and write shitty stories about my Minecraft persona to now. Thank you for reading my writing projects and standing behind me through every step of the process.

Thank you to every educator who encouraged me to write. If they hadn't told me that my writing was good, above average even, I wouldn't be writing these acknowledgments today.

And lastly, thank you to all those families I grew up beside in my hometown in Germany. Thank you, thank you for giving me a solid foundation and sticking around for me even as I navigate the rocky parts of life. Thank you to one boy in particular. Nico, thank you for giving me the experience of a soul's true bond before I knew what it was. I miss you. I love you forever. One day, I'll see you again in Heaven. Until then... I'll crack another Monster open for you. Thank you for every moment you managed to exist.

Keep fighting, all of you readers. Keep shining or crying or whatever you need to do, but keep fighting. One day, we will triumph over everything that hurt us

ABOUT THE AUTHOR

Regulus-Anthony Kelly (he/him) is a grandfather in the body of a teenage girl. Through wisdom and health issues, he's weathering the storms of life to bring his stories into the world. Currently, he is a rising Senior working to make it to college with a decent GPA. In his free time, he sketches characters on paper (the cover was one of his attempts at digital art!) and makes far too many playlists. He resides in Kansas, a far cry from his childhood in Germany, and works his way to crawling to Scotland.

You can find him on Instagram at reg.anthony.author, where he tries his best to only post professional content.